M000275566

Phe and the Work of Death

Mary R. H. Demmler

ISBN: 978-1-66781-858-0

Table of Contents

1 Phe

That's me, there, in the corner of the room. You'd have mistaken me for a pile of fluffy white towels, generic to any hotel room. It's time for me to rest, hidden in plain view, until the police and coroner finish their business. At this point, I'm always too tired to leave or take the next run. Over the years I've become an expert at finding forms more natural to the setting in order to hide, for on one of my first runs I mistakenly rested as a banana tree in a forest in Wales. That gave the locals a good puzzle.

My name is Phe, short for Phoenix but pronounced "Fay."

This run for me was pretty typical: I had come for an 83-year-old woman on holiday, visiting family. It was peaceful. The family had spent the past three days visiting and enjoying being together after five years of no visits. The kids were busy, the grandkids even more so, and the woman didn't like to travel alone. This time she made the extra effort, though, even ordering a car all on her own from the airport. This morning they walked along the shore and had ice cream for breakfast. The grandkids were delighted and the children shocked. This wasn't the mother they remembered. She was different, somehow, more playful.

She had come back to the hotel to take a nap before dinner. That's when I arrived. She lay down and closed her eyes for the last time. I floated near her, watching her spirit lift. The threads holding her soul to her body were turning silver as they gently broke.

I had manifested earlier in the week in order to travel with her to the shore. She was uncertain about the flight and I wanted to watch over her. I had chosen a manifestation that resembled a childhood friend of hers. We smiled at each other on the bus to the airport and then I managed to be in line three people ahead of her at the cafe. She smiled and waved, not really knowing why.

Not-so-miraculously we were seated next to each other on the plane. I introduced myself, deciding "Susanna" felt like a suitable name this time, and told her how much she reminded me of my grandmother, God rest her soul. In no time she was telling me about her childhood friend Susan and how much I reminded her of an adult version of this most beloved companion. I asked her to tell me more and the next two hours were filled with stories of giggling girls, first kisses, naked swims at the shore, and lost necklaces. She giggled and cried and apologized, "I don't know why I'm telling you all of these things, you, a perfect stranger. I haven't thought of them in years."

"That's okay," I told her, "I have that effect on people and I love to listen." She gave me a grateful smile; I suspected she felt I was indulging her.

At the end of the flight, we hugged at the gate. She cried again: confused, relieved, embarrassed, grateful. I told her it was a true pleasure and that I hoped to see her again. She didn't know then that I would come to her in four days' time.

The only thing I wondered about was why her husband hadn't made this run with me to be her companion. After twenty years of being apart, I would think he would want to be the first one she would see. Having never been married, or in love, or human, I can't begin to pretend to understand their emotions or reasoning. Truthfully, I find humans to be a bit of a novelty, a curiosity. I don't understand half of what they do but find them very entertaining. From what I knew, a safe assumption would be that her husband would come with me but no instructions were given to bring him along.

These are my favorite runs. There's no real sadness here. She spent the last six months packing her mementos, spending several minutes with each item, remembering the people and places that made them special. The rest of her belongings she had organized into piles to give away, to throw away, or to donate. As she travelled she had been aware that this was likely her last time seeing her family. She made sure to tell them how cherished they were, beautifully and wonderfully made. She had brought a special gift for each of them from her belongings, something she thought they would enjoy and keep. She was proud of herself, her children, her grandchildren, and her life.

As her soul lifted and she turned her face to me, she recognized me from the plane and whispered, "A familiar face." I smiled at her and took her arm. As I sent her on, ahead of her I could see a faint shadow—the husband. He had come after all.

2 The Tourist

Hawaii. It's been awhile since I made a run here. Truthfully, islanders are better at death than mainlanders. People more in touch with their history generally have healthier, more ancient traditions to usher the dying into the next realm and they tend to mourn in expressive and healthy ways. Americans from the mainland and visitors from Europe tend to judge the locals here and other islanders for their loud wailing at the loss of a loved one, but what they don't know is that the cries and shouts give wind to the sails of the dead, carrying them faster into the dimensions of the departed. There is deep love in their sorrow and, once the wailing is done, they feel the relief gained from the mourning. They don't feel the need to hold on as long as mainlanders do because they've allowed themselves to be as heartbroken as they feel, fueling the healing process.

I'm here for a tourist who is uncertain and scared. Usually they don't have much family around them so they become filled with concern and regret, wondering about loved ones thousands of miles away and how they will handle the death from such a distance.

I haven't arrived in any physical manifestation; I'm here to watch and wait. We may be born in the divine realm but that doesn't give us eternal consciousness. God formed us in the place where there is no time and set us to do work that serves the divine passion for showing great love and care for all of God's creation. In my case and that for all of the death and comforting presences, that means tending to humans in their most vulnerable moments. God loves humans deeply and made us to be with them when the divine presence is most needed. But we do not share God's all knowing essence. I do not know the exact moment when a soul will sever from the earthly plane. Moreover, I have no insight into the spiritual, mental, or emotional workings of humans. I try to fight against assumptions I have made about them over the centuries and dedicated my attention to doing just as my title indicates: be present.

Partly this is because the dying often make their own decisions about when to let go. We don't always know if we'll be needed to bring calm and peace in a time of uncertainty or if we'll be preparing the spirit of the dead for the gateway. There are occasions when we arrive and wait but are not yet needed. This happens in hospitals often. Many souls come close to death here then either the medical staff intervenes or the human's own body finds some way to heal and we aren't needed.

I find my tourist in the operating room. She's a woman from France on an extended holiday with her husband. The delicious duck she ate on the cruise and lavishly praised for its tenderness came with an unexpected surprise: a small sliver of bone that managed to navigate past her teeth, aimed straight for the lining of her stomach. Diagnosis: gastrointestinal perforation. She woke up with severe stomach pains. Luckily, the ship was coming into port and they were able to bring her directly here. The doctors are making their incision in an effort to pull out the sliver of bone and repair the tear.

I'm not here for the doctors, nurses, and hospital staff. They have others around them from our comforting division. I'm not sure what to call those others, or myself, for that matter. We aren't spirits. Spirits or souls are what we come to assist. Humans like to call us "angels," but that's entirely wrong. I don't want the angels' job and they don't want mine. That's a whole different department. I guess you could say I'm a presence. There are many of us and we all have different expertise and purposes. Me, I'm a death presence. The comforting presences are here to steady the doctors and nurses while I'm here for the patient. Again, I'm glad I don't have their job and they're very glad they don't have mine.

It looks like there are four comforting presences here today. This case must be more serious than I would have thought because they're focused on their work and barely look up when I enter. They aren't happy to see me. They know that since I'm here, death is near. The work of the comforting presences might need to change. If she doesn't make it through the surgery and off the operating table, they will have to shift gears and prepare the medical team for the confusion, disappointment, and questions that come after such a death. I know not to take it personally.

The surgeons frantically try to save the tourist, but she's starting to crash. I see her spirit float up and turn to look down at her body. The spirit is startled and afraid to see her abdomen split open and bleeding. It must be a shock for them to see themselves like this. I make my way over to her and place my hand on her shoulder. The Tourist turns to see me, confused, then relieved. She knows she's not alone in here and wraps her arm around me. I smile at her and try to surround her with my energy.

She looks up at me with peaceful eyes that quickly open wide with surprise. Her heart stopped beating while the surgeons made their last stitch and now they have the paddles on her chest, charged and ready. The crack of lightning enters her body as the doctor yells, "Clear!" In a flash her spirit is pulled back into her body as the tourist's heart starts up again. The other presences reach out to place hands on the shoulders of the medical team members to share in their relief and to give them a little more strength to finish.

I stay in the hospital for the next few days, overhearing the words "touch and go" batted around from doctors and nurses to the husband and then by the husband on the phone to all of the relatives.

"Hey, Sabine. Good to see you." I say to the comforting presence that has drifted into the room.

"Oui. Good to see you, too."

Sabine is here for the husband. She will sit with him for the next few days as he watches his wife struggle and then become stable again. We've worked together a lot and I really like her. She's easy to be around, doesn't talk too much, and is diligent in her duties. She was one of the few who managed to stay through the entire Black Death pandemic. The death presences had no choice but to work the duration of the plague - too much death for us to take shifts. But the comforting presences could trade off some in order to recharge. Not Sabine. She stayed and moved from family member to family member as one after another fell.

We worked several households together during those exhausting days. I remember one particularly painful family. I started the grandmother on her journey, then turned around to prepare for the infant grandchild the next day. I crumpled and rested as a stack of hay in the corner, knowing the rest of the family would fall victim due to their exhaustion and grief. Sabine stayed until the last of the nine family members, a 12-year-old son, made his departure. Ever since then I've been relieved whenever we make a run together. We both know we've seen worse and can manage most cases now with genuine ease and kinship between us.

The tourist stays unconscious for fifty-two hours but her spirit never rises again. I can tell she's in there, hearing the husband as he reads her that morning's edition of Le Figaro on his tablet. She also listens as he snores from his chair, having not left her side since she came out of surgery. The ragged sounds of his breathing bring her comfort as her body tries to heal.

As the husband sleeps, Sabine fills me in on her own travels. When shots rang out in Sandy Hook Elementary School, Sabine responded immediately. She consistently works during and after major tragedies, like Sandy Hook, and stays for months, sometimes years. In that situation, with it occurring at Christmas time, she faithfully travelled home to home to home without taking breaks. She stayed through Easter but I've seen her work nonstop for longer. Since then she's been around the world multiple times to minister in volatile areas. Wars, mass shootings, genocide, these are the things that make even the best of us question how our God could love humans so deeply. But never once have I heard Sabine question or complain, only ever work with delicate care and compassion.

"You know the woman in Wales a few weeks back?" Sabine says, "The one in the hotel room? I made the run to her family. That was a good one. No one was heartbroken; sad, but not heartbroken. They talked about how happy she had been and uncharacteristically playful. She told her kids all about the young woman on the plane next to her, and how the young woman had listened as the widow went on and on, sharing childhood memories. Nice work."

I look at Sabine with a grin. "Thanks. I had the luxury of time with that one and I couldn't help but take advantage. She was lovely. I got to listen to her giggle like a child again and see her face light up. I was a little surprised she didn't mention her husband and I was very surprised he didn't make the full run with me."

Sabine looked at me then away. "Phe, when I was with the family, I listened to their good memories of her but heard few mentions of him. Only after the funeral did the daughters-in-law speak with one another about him. They wondered what the widow's and the husband's reunion might be like, since he had died the day before he was planning to leave the family for his mistress."

"All of these years and I still don't get it—these human complexities baffle me. I didn't see the family, but that widow was marvelous. How anyone would want to leave her is beyond my understanding."

Sabine and I sit in silence only for a moment. The tourist slowly opens her eyes and speaks her husband's name with a raspy, dry voice. He wakes from his nap and jumps up to be by her side, tears of relief streaming down his face. Between the medical interventions and her body's desire to heal, she'll be fine now, so I look at Sabine and give her a nod.

Earlier in the day I thought the Tourist's crisis had ended and I could leave but I stayed to spend time with Sabine. She's one of the old ones and it is good to spend time with an old friend. I suppose we all have days when even presences need some companionship.

Sabine will have another day or two still with the couple, but my work is done. I smile at her one last time and say, "Thanks." She smiles back then turns her loving attention back to the Tourist and her husband.

3 The Salesman

I've been hanging around a hospital in Texas for a couple of days now. This run dropped me in the middle of the Texas hill country in August. By the looks of everyone around me, the heat must be bad. I know I'm here for the Salesman, but this extreme heat might demand an extra run or two of me while I'm here.

The Salesman has COPD and now pneumonia. They have a full mask on him to force the oxygen into his lungs. The hope is that his oldest daughter will make it here from Oregon to be by his side with her two younger sisters before he dies. The youngest lives locally and is the Salesman's primary caregiver; the middle daughter arrived yesterday from Houston. She talks about how the heat is even worse back home and the two daughters argue over which city is the hottest.

Sibling rivalry is another thing I can't get my head around: why exactly do human siblings compete all the time? I see it often in rooms like this one. The nervous and worried energy overwhelms them so they find past events and old arguments to bicker about. The energy has to be released somehow. It's always stupid stuff like the weather on a beach vacation 30 years ago, or whose dog was better behaved when they were kids, or which one caught the bigger trout that one time they went camping. It's like a verbal version of the guy who won't stop shaking his leg when he's sitting down: that energy has to come out somehow.

Griffin is here to tend the sisters. He's another one of my friends among the comforting presences. The two women start up again. He looks at me and rolls his eyes before resting a hand on each of their shoulders. They settle down and the middle daughter decides to text the older sister to see if she's landed and made it to her rental car.

I nod at Griffin and slip out of the room. The Salesman isn't going any time soon. This kind of death comes with choices. The Salesman is waiting for something, but he's the only one who can name what that is and even he doesn't know it yet. Maybe it's the arrival of the oldest daughter; maybe it's a chance to say something to all three girls; maybe he wants to hear the daughters say they love each other one last time—there's no way to know.

I have a feeling his wife will appear when time gets closer. She died when the youngest daughter was just a year old. I remember because I was the one who made that run. She was heartbroken. The mom didn't want to leave her girls and the Salesman but she had no choice. The doctors put her on bed rest when she was pregnant with their last daughter. No one knew it, but she had developed a blood clot in her leg. One day when she was out playing with her girls, the clot moved and travelled to her lungs, a pulmonary embolism. There was no way the doctors could have known, and no way she could have felt it coming. One moment she was pushing the middle daughter in the swing in the yard and the next she was lying on the lawn. The oldest daughter ran to the neighbor's to call the ambulance. I watched as the mother's spirit rose up from her body and registered deep emotional pain. We floated there, watching the girls fall on top of the mother's body. The neighbors had to lift them off of her so the paramedics could try in vain to revive her.

I find an empty stairwell and manifest into a form similar to that of a former coworker of the Salesman: a woman who answered the phone on the floor. He doesn't know that she passed away a year ago in Dallas. He had liked her and even thought about asking her out, but he couldn't reconcile sharing his attention with her and his daughters. His girls always came first, no matter what. He had worked hard to become mother and father to them. He learned to braid hair and managed to pay for braces and most of college for all three of them.

The only thing he allowed for himself was his cigarettes, a small indulgence that only took 2-3 minutes but helped take the edge off of his worry. Between breaks from the floor, drinks with clients, and a couple of cigarettes after getting the girls bathed and to bed every night, the Salesman had worked up to a pack-a-day habit. And now it was going to take him from the daughters who had been the center of his life.

I knock on the Salesman's door and the daughters invite me in. "I'm Tiffany," I say. "I'm Barb's daughter. Mom worked with your dad at the dealership and she asked me to look in on him. She heard he was in the hospital." I act a little nervous and unsure so that the daughters will open up. It works.

"Come on in. . . Tiffany, did you say?"

"Yes. Thank you. I won't stay long."

"No! We welcome the company, especially from someone connected to Daddy's work. He loved his job and the people he worked with at the shop. I think I remember meeting your mom once. Dark hair? Blue eyes?"

"That's her! Big eyes and bigger hair. And lots of jewelry! She wears a ring on every finger."

The daughters giggle. They remember Barb. She loved to tell kids jokes that were a little too mature for them and the girls still find them hilarious.

I step over to the Salesman and smile. His eyes brighten up, even under his mask. He recognizes the resemblance but doesn't know quite who I am, only that my face is somehow comforting. He reaches his hand out from under his hospital sheet. I take it and give it a squeeze then wink at him. He smiles again, then turns his head away. He's tired.

I step back and prop myself on the window sill behind the daughters' chairs. Hospital rooms seem to get smaller and smaller. I don't especially enjoy spending time in them in my manifest form. I'd rather be free to float and linger.

After some small talk followed by silence, the daughters settle back into remembering childhood trips and fretting over their sister's arrival. We hear a knock on the door and the daughters perk up, hoping it's their sister.

"Come in!" they almost shout.

"Oh, it's you Dr. Markham," the younger daughter says.

"Sorry to disappoint," the doctor says in a tender and caring voice. After centuries of being in sick rooms, I'm still adjusting to seeing female doctors.

"No, please. We're just waiting for our sister. She's flying in from Oregon this afternoon. She should be here any minute."

"I see. I'm glad she's coming. I know your father will be glad to have you all in the same room again. And who are you?" She's looking at me. Honestly, I had forgotten that I was manifest and they could see me.

"My apologies. My name is Tiffany. I'm the daughter of an old friend."

"Nice to meet you. Do you mind stepping out while I visit with the patient and his family?"

"No. Of course. I was about to leave anyway. I just had promised Mama I'd look in on them. It was nice meeting all of you." I step into the waiting room, trying to decide whether or not to change forms again. I choose to stay manifest for selfish reasons. There's a Coke machine in the waiting room and a cold Coca-Cola is my indulgence, maybe the only one I have. The machine drops one down just as I walk up to it. I grab the can and listen for the pop and hiss as I pull the top. Now this, this is one thing about humans I can understand.

As I sit down to enjoy my personal vice, the doctor pops her head in.

"Tiffany, is it?" I have to think for a moment. I'm not always good at remembering the stories I create for myself.

"Yes!" I say a little too loudly. "I'm Tiffany. The daughter of a friend."

"Yes, you said. Were your mother and Mr. Sanchez good friends?"

"They were. They worked together for years." I sincerely hope she doesn't ask me many more questions. I don't think I have the creative energy to make it any more detailed.

"Tell your mom she made good friends. Mr. Sanchez has been a good patient, as in the real meaning of the word, always joking, even on the worst days. Even now he's being pretty amazing."

"Thanks, Dr. Markham, I'll let her know."

"Please, call me Anne. I get the feeling you're not local, so I don't expect I'll be seeing you as a patient."

"Anne. Mother of Mary. Grandmother of Jesus." I say.

"That's right. Few people around here know that."

She must have a great rapport with her patients. We've been sitting here for two minutes and she already has me engaged.

"It's nice to meet you, Anne. Thank you for taking the time to speak with me and for being, obviously, a great doctor. The work you do matters, more than you can know."

"Thanks. Sometimes it doesn't feel like it." She looks down and I can see she's tired.

"Trust me, I'm an expert. Keep up the good work."

She looks at me a little strangely, then smiles before I walk out of the waiting room. I leave my perfectly good Coke behind, but I can't stay with Anne any longer. Something pulls me away, tells me to leave her.

I step out of the hospital into the Texas sun and breathe in the hot air one last time before slipping out of my manifest form. I'll be better off being able to float around the room. This is going to be a long night and Griffin and I will need all the room we can get. The third sister has just arrived and behind her I see a comforting presence that I don't recognize. By the end of the night we'll know each other pretty well. If she's travelling with the daughter, then that means the daughter is hurting.

All night we watch over the Salesman and his daughters. His blood pressure and pulse drop. The nurses hear the alarms from the machines, then rush in with their implements and carts, just in time to watch his body claw its way back up to more stable levels. He does this again and again. The daughters chat, take turns sleeping, panic every time he seems to be declining, and hold each other.

Around four a.m. the Salesman makes a motion with his hands and scratches a note on a piece of paper held up for him by the middle daughter. The youngest sees what's written on the page and bolts out the door. The other two women look at each other, confused. Griffin stays in the room with the other comforting presence. I learn that her name is Mariah and she's relatively new. This is her 543rd run. Griffin knows the younger daughter is in the best condition, having been the one who has spent the most time with the Salesman, so doesn't go with her.

A half hour later the daughter returns, carrying something. "Daddy, I found them. It took me a minute because I couldn't remember where I'd seen it, but then I remembered your nightstand." She reaches out and places a scratched up Zippo lighter in the Salesman's hand. He smiles, then closes his eyes and sighs.

It's time. The wife arrives along with the spirit of a young man in army fatigues. I get it now: the Salesman suffers from survivor's guilt. The Salesman looks at each of his girls in turn, then straight at his wife and his army buddy, both of whom had died long before him and he had never learned to deal with either death. He nods and closes his eyes, sucking in one last deep breath. He opens his eyes long enough to catch mine and smiles, nods, and exhales.

The daughters fall on the Salesman's body, the same as they had their mother's all those years before. Like their mother, the Salesman floats above them, full of pride and love and heartbreak. He's tired and he's ready. I do my job, watching as he journeys between his wife and his friend.

This time I collapse in the form of a worn lab coat on the back of a chair behind the nurses' station. I'm close enough to the charts that I can listen to Dr. Markham--Anne. I find her voice soothing as she talks herself through the notes she makes. She records the steps they took to make the Salesman comfortable and that they had decided not to attempt to revive him, per the daughters' wishes and her own best judgment.

Griffin left Mariah tending to the daughters so he could stand next to Anne and near the nurses. He knows Anne is grieving for the daughters and places a hand on her shoulder as a tear drops on the chart beneath her. He spots me out of the corner of his eye, crumpled on the back of the chair. He grins and nods.

4 The Teenager

If you look up the trunk of a tall pine tree to your right, you'll find me sitting on a limb way up in the canopy. This is east Tennessee and the Appalachian mountains are giving their best fall show. It's one of my favorite places to be this time of year. The mountains look like God threw one of the giant patchwork quilts common in this part of the world over the humps and valleys of the ridges.

I came early to watch nightfall. If I'm sent on a late night run during football season to a back road in the mountains, then it's pretty certain I'm here for a teenager. This one will be tough and will take some time, so I'm taking my time to enjoy the peace before the storm of sorrow.

I love the stillness and bathe in it as long as I can. There's a sweetness in the arrival of the cold air that sweeps in as the sun sweeps out. Around 11 p.m. an owl perches next to me. He can see me. Owls have long been our companions around the world. They are the watchers of the night and keepers of the dark. In this region, the older people say that the sound of a screech owl at night is a warning that death is near. They fail to recognize that death is always near. The owl makes no sound but turns his head to look at me then back down the road.

At 1:43 a.m. we hear the tires. We're perched in a sharp switchback turn that cuts through these mountains and can hear the truck's speed. This one will be violent and sudden, loud and confusing. It is why I waited here in the turn of the road. It's better if I'm here to catch the spirit at such a sudden separation rather than riding along with him. Or maybe I'm tired of witnessing the extreme change in emotion and circumstance for souls such as these. Those are the sounds of a truck driven by a young person who is full of life and invincibility, only aware of the rush of driving fast after a great Friday night under the stadium lights.

The owl turns to look at me one last time before flying off. He'll screech once he reaches his next perch, a call to signal death has come to the mountains.

The truck barely slows as it leaves the road. The night is dark, a new moon, and the teenager didn't have the twists and turns memorized as well as he assumed. Simultaneously I hear the crunch of metal as the engine wraps around a tree and the shattering of glass as the boy's body flies through the front windshield. As his body hits a distant tree, his spirit rips away. I can hear the severing, the tearing of threads fast and harsh. He was strong and young and his spirit was tied closely with his body. This was sudden and unexpected and violent.

I pause for a moment, one last moment of quiet. The forest is still again and I take it in before floating down to the Teenager. His spirit is utterly confused and panicked, it tries to rush back to the body now mangled by the tree.

I follow. Grabbing him won't serve any purpose now. He must see and try to process for himself. It's horrible for him, to see his invincible self unrecognizable and realizing he is floating next to it. His spirit swirls with chaotic energy. Then I see it shift as understanding puts order to it again. That's when I reach out and lightly touch his shoulder. He turns to me, not surprised but full of questions.

I float him back up to the tree branch where the owl had kept me company. We look down on the wreckage and sit in silence again. I'm in no rush. No one knows the Teenager would have come this way. He took a friend home after the game, which took him away from his usual route. It will be hours before the graveyard shift leaves the factory down in the valley, sending the next drivers on this road. Even then, several will pass until the light of early dawn increases enough for anyone to see the truck and then more time will pass as they travel over the mountain to where there is cell service again.

The Teenager sits silent for a long time. I'm surprised, actually. Usually the questions and anger have started by now, especially with one his age. He just sits and looks at his truck below us and his body nearby. Finally, he turns to me and asks,

"What does he need me for?"

I'm confused. "What?"

"What does he need me for?"

"Who? Who needs you? I don't understand."

"God. What does he need me for?"

Ah. I've heard this before but the concept still leaves me dumbfounded. The Teenager doubtlessly has been told that when someone dies it's because, "God needs them in heaven more than we need them here on earth."

Several of us have talked about this but still don't understand it. Why would God need any human in the divine realm? Why would she suddenly take humans from their families, causing such pain, out of some need to have them with her? I really don't understand it. It sounds so arrogant to me and the others that humans would assume God would need them somehow and that she would selfishly rip them from their lives to have them with her.

The tendency of humans to refer to God as "he," I understand. Thanks to Jesus' teaching on the Trinity, very well done I might add, Christians have always called God "he." Truthfully, God is neither male nor female but we presences tend to refer to God however we refer to ourselves. I'm a "she" so God is a "she." Important for us is whatever brings us comfort and opens us more fully to God, whatever deepens our trust and understanding.

But how does thinking God "needs" a human in the divine realm comfort loved ones when one is ripped from them?

I look at the teenager. "No. That's not what's happening. God doesn't need you for anything. God loves you and has never left you, but you didn't die because God 'needs' you for some purpose. You had plenty of purpose here."

"Then why? Why would he take me from all of this? Why now?!"

I feel the anger start to rise inside the Teenager. It doesn't bother me and I'm not afraid of it. The anger is natural and understandable, especially for one still so young and full of life. I can feel the anxiety and fear as well that follow whenever humans become angry with God. Generally they don't trust her enough to share their anger with her. Many of them don't understand how anger opens the way for relationship, understanding, and healing. All of us go through a time of anger with our work, since our entire being revolves around death and ushering souls fully into her. It's difficult work and the anger is a necessary step in our deepening relationship with God, but also in forging a greater capacity for compassion for those with whom we work.

It will take time for the Teenager to understand. He has his own passages through anger and sadness, regret and fear, ahead of him. But they all lead to the same opening and freedom, the same ultimate joy from belonging.

I take his hand in mine as we sit and I hold it for a moment. He allows me some silence as I allow his anger to settle. Anger is always a symptom of something deeper, so I wait for his sadness to take its true form.

"You died. That's it. You weren't paying attention and drove too fast on a mountain road. It's physics, really, which I know is of little comfort right now. You drove too fast and it was too dark and that's it. The truck came off the road and hit the tree, sending your body flying. The impact with the tree was too much to take and your spirit separated from your physical form."

He sits with this for a moment. I feel the guilt arrive and I can't do anything to stop it. Young or old, most humans must pass through guilt before letting themselves be free. They want to make their death their fault, as if taking responsibility now will somehow change things. The Salesman did the same. He shamed himself over the cigarettes he smoked and the doctor's appointments he missed. I've heard it all before: "I should have," "I shouldn't have," "If only I had." All I can do is be present with them but my heart breaks for the ease with which humans reach for shame, on themselves and others.

"If God needed you in heaven and pulled you from your family like this, truthfully, that would make God very selfish, would it not? To inflict such deep pain of loss on your family because he needs you in some way? Especially a god whom we all know is all powerful? Don't you pray, 'Almighty God'?"

The Teenager thinks for a moment, looking down the road. He's looking to where his family is, far in the distance somewhere, just starting to wonder why he hasn't come home yet. His mother is beginning to worry and his father is fussing that he's probably hanging out with some of the other football players and lost track of time.

"I never thought about it that way. I suppose you're right. I guess I just assumed God knew better than I did..."

I laugh slightly, "Well, that much is true: God does know better than all of us. But that doesn't mean God makes things happen. He watches and loves and sits with us all through the pain but doesn't cause it. That would make God malicious and mean, and I can tell you for certain that isn't the case."

"So what now?" the Teenager asks. "Where's the bright light? The hymns and clouds and stuff?"

"Now it's up to you. I can take you whenever you're ready. We can sit and wait for them to find you or you can go on, whichever you feel you need."

"That's it? No big sound? No 'heavenly voices?' Was everything I was taught a lie?!"

The anger starts to come back. Fear this time is the real emotion and I get it. He thought he knew how it would be and now he's finding out that it's not. I take his hand again and look at him.

"Everything you were taught wasn't a lie. The people who tried to teach you about and show you God, they were doing the best they could and shared with you what they thought they knew. They didn't lie to you."

"But what next? What happens to me?! Where am I going?! Oh, God! I'm not going . . .you know . . . to HELL am I?!" (Another conceptual love affair I wish humans would quit.)

I put my arm around him to quiet him. "No! No. You're fine. Wait. Settle."

I hope that his spirit will calm down and let go but the agitation and fear are too strong, so I tell him what I have come to understand.

"No. You're fine. And you're loved. That's first. That's always first. I'm willing to bet you know the song, 'Jesus Loves Me,' right?"

He nods his head with questions still large in his eyes.

"Ok. Then you know the most important part. And you know that the people who taught you this song loved you very much, right? Your parents and grandparents? Your Sunday School teachers?"

He nods some more, waiting.

"I've been around a long time. For centuries I've been doing this work."

Surprise crosses his face and I smile at him.

"Even I don't understand it all and sometimes I struggle with that. I wish I knew. I wish I could tell you every detail of every step and could answer every question you have. But God is too big. Too big even for me and certainly too big for you or any other human to comprehend. In fact, God is so big that all the humans together still aren't close to understanding."

I look at him to see how he's doing. He's listening intently, wanting to comprehend what I'm saying.

"But humans don't do well with mystery, not generally. You all like to test and dig and research and theorize and answer. It's actually one of the things God gave you that she loves the most—he loves the most. You don't do well with questions to which there are no answers. But with God, there are more questions than answers and that's the way it's meant to be. That doesn't prevent humans from still wanting certainty. All of those people who love you and taught you everything you know, they wanted to give you answers and they wanted to give themselves answers. So they said what they thought made sense and what brought them comfort."

Listening to myself I start to grow uncomfortable. Am I doing what the humans do? Trying to provide answers so the Teenager won't feel as afraid or uncertain? Where is my own faith? My own belief? I know what comes next is beyond my comprehension, so what business do I have trying to tell the Teenager anything? But I also know that what comes next is pure love and I want to convey that in some way to this young spirit. I realize, in this moment, maybe I've come to love humans some too. This surprises me as I sit on the branch with him.

"I think I'm ready." The Teenager's voice pulls me from my own questioning. "I don't want to wait any longer. If love is what waits, that will be better than seeing friends or family find me."

It's my turn to nod in understanding. He's young enough to still trust what I have said without needing further proof. I pull him close and we start the transition.

Once I know he's calm and moved on, I come back to the scene. I crumple like a piece of metal possibly thrown into the woods by the collision. I want to rest with the Teenager's questions and see who comes with the police and ambulance. This is a small town and every person who answers the emergency call will have known the Teenager or his family in some way. At least one will be a cousin or a brother or an aunt.

I hear the sirens climb the mountain roads and watch as my comforting friends arrive, bringing with them some new faces ready to learn how to respond to this kind of death. They wait, then fly to the emergency personnel as they leave their vehicles and start comprehending what happened and putting together the pieces. Again I'm glad I don't have the comforting presences' job and they are glad they don't have mine. I can calm a departing spirit and answer their questions, but I don't know how to sit with the shock and pain of those left behind, feeling helpless by not being able to offer answers but only able to sit, to be a presence.

5 The Visitor

I've made my way to a small hospital in Vermont, this time the pediatric ward. Don't worry, I'm not here for one of the young ones. I'm hovering in the hallway for the Visitor who soon will step off the elevator. I volunteered for this one. I was mentoring our new death presence, Genevieve, when she made a run for someone connected to him. Nine years have passed, which is a mere moment for me but feels so long ago for him. Honestly, it feels like a long time ago for me too. I think I'm tired.

The elevator bell rings and out steps the Visitor, a large smile on his face as he carries his signature rainbow bag slung over his shoulder. Buttons cover the long multicolor handles with sayings like, "You got this!" "Your smile makes my day!" and "Dream and Believe." I know that the bright shining smile he wears now only appeared as the doors opened. He limits himself to feeling his overwhelming sadness during the minute and a half elevator ride. Once those doors open, he becomes a different person.

The blocked artery going to his heart should have killed him yesterday but he doesn't know that. He's a walking miracle. Those of us who have worked this hospital with him have watched anxiously. We wanted him to have more time for this last trip to the ward, this last half hour doing what he has loved.

I float behind him and watch him work. Every week he comes to this hallway, bag in hand, to check on each patient. It's a small hospital with a small pediatrics department. It doesn't take long and usually the kids here aren't terminal but recovering. The more serious cases are sent to the children's hospitals in one of the bigger cities nearby. These kids have had tonsils removed, bad breaks set in casts, or are recovering from a bad case of the flu; things like that.

The Visitor stops at the door of every room. He says a brief prayer of gratitude before he enters. Incredibly, this work brings him life and he is thankful to be here week in and week out. As he takes his first step into a room, the same smile returns to his face that first appeared as he stepped off the elevator. His voice rises to a mellifluous tone and the whole room brightens with his presence. He'll spend a little time with each kid, telling them a joke and giving them a new stuffed animal. He always has the right one in his bag for each young patient. This is one of his gifts. When he packs before leaving the house, he looks at his inventory of miscellaneous toys and chooses exactly the ones the kids will want without knowing any of the children he'll meet that day.

I watch him repeat his ritual seven times as he goes down the hallway today. The nurses pass and smile, thanking him for being there. On two of his stops, parents follow him into the hallway as he leaves their child's room in order to shake his hand and tell him how much he has brightened their child's day. He has made this place a little less frightening for all of them. He always smiles and nods, never saying a word.

After he leaves the last room, he completes his ritual with a treat for himself: a trip to the vending machines tucked inside the family waiting room. Every week it's the same. He looks at the machine, pretending to choose, as if he would buy anything other than the black and white snack cake wrapped in thin cellophane. He likes the way the icing coats the inside of his mouth, the same as it has helped coat the inside of his arteries all these years.

As he stands, staring at his choices, I see Genevieve arrive with a small soul. She has returned with the Visitor's daughter, the soul she helped transition nine years ago. I join them, taking the other hand of the small soul, knowing she will be eager to go to her father's spirit when the time comes. But these moments are unpredictable. I never know how these cases will play out. After the daughter left with Genevieve nine years ago, the parents couldn't hold their lives together anymore. They divorced and the Visitor struggled to get out of bed in the morning, much less work. It wasn't until he started these visits that his life began again, altered but with a new purpose.

I hear the Visitor press the buttons and know the moment has come. As the machine whirs to release his selection, his body starts to fall. The blockage has stopped the flow of blood to his heart and he collapses. His soul rips from his body before it even hits the floor. He can't wait any longer to be free and restored. The threads stretch, then snap, in his eagerness as he lunges for his daughter. Genevieve and I let go and he snatches her soul up into his, both spirits intertwined in a dance of joy. It is nothing short of beautiful. Moments like these I almost sense what tears must feel like.

There's really no work for us now. Genevieve supervises as the daughter helps the Visitor transition. There is only happiness here and ease, so I decide to stay in the waiting room, neatly folded in the form of a pamphlet on a table. I'm happier, too, but still tired. I watch as a member of the housekeeping staff finds the Visitor and cries out. Soon "Code Blue" echoes down the hallways from the intercom system and medical staff rushes in. All they know is how much they love and admire the Visitor and they want to help him any way they can. They don't understand he is healed and more whole now than he has been in nine years.

6 The Landowner

I've been at a plush hospice house outside Denver for nearly a week. Every room has a picture window with an unobstructed view of the Rockies. Every bed is positioned either next to the window or facing it, allowing the patients to look out onto the mountains. The rooms have no institutional feel to them. The firm that owns this house has decorated each room with antiques and beautiful accents. Today, that includes me: I'm the needlepoint pillow on the overstuffed armchair in the corner.

I could leave. My work has been done for hours but I'm taking some personal time to linger. This has been a particularly beautiful run and I'm not ready to leave this room.

The Landowner is—was—in his nineties. He's been living in this home for six months now, enjoying the view and the company of his wife and daughter. They've been by his side every day, tending to him and reading to him from the local newspaper and his worn copy of *Leaves of Grass*.

Hospice homes make for the easiest and most beautiful runs. No one working in hospice suffers from any delusions of being a rescuer or a miracle worker. They all know why they're here and what they are facing. It's why you find, quite often, the most spiritually grounded and humble doctors, nurses, and staff in hospice homes. On a fundamental level they know they work in one of the thin places of the human world, where the membrane between this physical realm and the eternal is barely intact.

The Landowner danced back and forth across that membrane while I was in the room with him and his family. He could see me. He wasn't anxious or scared but he wasn't in a hurry to leave. I have heard humans talk about a window of time when they're waking up from a night's sleep. They mention a weird thought or a great idea that came to them right as they were in that space between sleeping and wakefulness. I imagine that is what this week has been like for the Landowner. The hospice setting, because it is relaxed and non-anxious, gives spirits a chance to float in and out of bodies. More than in any other setting, hospice gives souls time to enjoy the thin place between death and the dimension of the departed.

I love watching some souls linger and almost play as they float in and out of their bodies. The moments around death are too sacred and special for words. No human language has succeeded in describing it. I've heard the term "baptism" and I think that might come close. After witnessing the violence of the Teenager's death, this passing comes as a balm to my own spirit.

The Landowner immersed himself in his time between last breaths and new dimensions. At one and the same time it seemed he was ready to be rid of his body but not quite ready to leave his wife and daughter. I wasn't ready for him to either. Inasmuch as I understand love, this family shared it on a deep and intimate level. The mother and daughter were able to sit for hours on end in silence, but not in any uncomfortable way. It was a silence filled with reconciliation, devotion, and intimacy. They didn't fill the space with words because they didn't need to. The space around them was filled with memories and love and hours already lived together.

Once or twice a day, one of the comforting presences would drop in to check on the family. I would spot them out the window, coming across the mountains. They acknowledged me, and then took their post behind the daughter or wife. After an hour or so they would turn to me.

"Hey, Phe. Have they been like this the whole time?"

"Pretty much. I've only been here a few days but I heard the nurses saying how faithful and devoted the wife and daughter have been. Apparently they've been here every day for months."

"There doesn't seem to be much need for me today," each of them would tell me.

"No," I would respond, "these two have each other pretty well covered."

I watched as each comforting presence stayed for a minute or two longer before drifting down the hall to check in other rooms to see if they might be needed by another family or hospice staff member.

Three times during my week the priest came by to see the family and pray over the Landowner. She wore the traditional black shirt with a white tab collar and would fit in with any training class as a new comforting presence. I noticed the Landowner, wife, and daughter all relax and take slightly deeper breaths when she entered. After centuries of only seeing men, I still am surprised by women in black shirts with white collars, similar to adjusting to seeing female doctors. But I like them. The souls of humans are varied and need just as wide a variety of holy people to tend them.

It was during the priest's third visit that the Landowner finally let go completely. I think he was waiting for a moment when his family wouldn't be watching and when there would be a friendly face in the room. The priest and daughter were talking about the view of the mountains and the wife started a story about a funny and nearly disastrous family outing. The Landowner had packed his wife and daughter in their station wagon when the daughter was very small. He had failed to fill the gas tank and the car stalled in the middle of Rocky Mountain National Park. Apparently a bull moose became a little too fascinated by the car while the family waited for help.

The wife spun the story so richly that I almost missed the Landowner's last breath. I noticed him rising again from his body, but this time his threads severed completely. I didn't go to him. Instead, he came to rest beside me and took my hand. We stayed and finished listening to the story.

"My family," he said, and squeezed my hand. "They made my life a Technicolor masterpiece."

Just as he turned again to look at his wife, the priest looked at the Landowner. She knew he was gone. She had sensed it only moments after he came to rest by me.

"I think it's time to get the nurse," she said to the daughter in a gentle voice. The daughter looked at the Landowner, then stood and went to his side, placing a hand on his chest. She dipped her head then turned to her mother and nodded.

"I'm ready," the Landowner said as he nearly led me into the next phase of his passage.

I finished my work and collapsed where I am now. No one noticed one more needlepoint throw pillow in the room and the chair was comfortable and inviting. I sat there, listening to the silence between the mother and the daughter as they tenderly held each other and the Landowner's hands. The nurse came in to verify his passing and then called the mortuary. The mother and daughter changed the Landowner out of his worn cotton pajamas and into a new pair, ones that still seemed comfortable but were more befitting of a man of his stature. Even in death they were tending to his needs.

All of them have left the room now but I'm not ready. Moments like these get me as close as I have ever been to understanding humans and what love must be for them. For a brief moment I envy them—even the Landowner.

7 The Clock Maker's Daughter

After the Landowner's body is taken away, I shift and drift out into the gardens of the hospice house. Water bubbles and sings as it flows over the rocks in the fountain. The sounds make a melody over the rhythm of the patients' breathing inside the house. From here I can watch my fellow death presences as they float in and out of the rooms, checking on their spirits and greeting the team of comforting presences that stay in the home for the families and the staff.

We don't often have the chance to watch one another work. When I see other spirits showing up, I know it means more than one death and work for all of us. We focus on the spirits whose departure has called us, so we have little time to turn and see others at work. Each of us tends the souls in our care in slightly different and beautiful ways and I feel pride in watching the others working in the house. I helped train each of them. There aren't many left who have been making runs as long as I have, even fewer who have been doing it longer. I'm glad to see the traditions of our work and identity being honored by the presences inside the home today.

Giving myself this time to watch my peers and friends gives my mind time to think back over the past few months. I've been busy and generally don't stop to reflect often. But I find this garden and the work of my friends invite me to spend some time contemplating.

I think back over the spirits I've assisted and the places I've been. One face keeps reappearing: Anne, the doctor from Texas.

Sitting here opens my eyes to the reason she feels familiar to me. I've been surprised to see her face come to my mind in the runs I've made since the Salesman. This is very unusual for me and I find it a bit unsettling. I've never much remembered secondary people to my work- family members, yes, but not others. Watching my friends work from my view in the hospice house garden sent my mind back and it came together for me. She reminds me of Árdghal, one of the ancient ones and one of my mentors. He had the same empathy and shine in his eyes as Anne, something I've been missing.

Most of us make our runs with a sense of duty and care, understanding our vocation and purpose, but Árdghal approached it with strong compassion and a dedication unmatched by any other presence I have known. With passion he made his runs to every battlefield, every field of famine, every plague, determined that the souls should encounter something better, something more beautiful in this realm before passing on to the next. Redemption and resurrection were his mantras as he led us all to shepherd at the worst deaths humans could conjure up.

Side by side we worked Dachau for the duration of the humans' second great war. Some spirits we grabbed before the SS officers even unloaded the trains. Others we followed for only a few hours as they were processed and marched directly to the horrific chambers. Still others we watched for weeks, months, even years, as their bodies nearly disappeared before their souls could escape.

Soon after Dachau opened, Árdghal and I followed the family of a clockmaker. Upon their arrival, Árdghal cradled the first soul of that family—an infant who died of fever within hours of being unloaded from the train. One by one we attended to nearly all nine of the family members, carrying away the mother, grandmother, and almost all of the children in turn.

The clockmaker himself was a strong and capable man. Together with his two sons he was put to work in the camps. The time came when he held each of his boys as they died, and watched their bodies being thrown on a wagon with the rest of the empty and expended shells. Árdghal would collapse after every one of his runs near the clockmaker. There was something about this man that Árdghal respected and admired. I think he saw in the clockmaker the same profound integrity and passion that burned inside himself.

Three weeks before that terrible war's end, the clockmaker ran out of fire in his heart that pushed him to survive and the threads of his soul broke loose from his body. Árdghal insisted on making the run himself. I watched as he lovingly reached out to take the clockmaker's hand, two kindred spirits connecting. The clockmaker looked up at him and said, "Old friend. My turn." I knew then that he had been able to see Árdghal for some time. I think it was because of the constant nearness of death in the camps. But perhaps it was something more, a deeper kinship between the two that brought a special kind of sight.

Three weeks later the war ended and over the next year we watched the survivors of the camp find new homes. Among them was the last of the clockmaker's family, a fourteen-year-old daughter. Like her father she had a spirit of fire that had pushed her to live, working with bloodied hands but an unbloodied soul throughout her time in the camp.

The clockmaker's daughter eventually went to college and graduate school, studying the history of her people and becoming a professor in a large university. She wanted others to learn of the atrocities of the camps but also how beauty rises from ashes in the form of art and literature produced by former prisoners. Árdghal would check in on her now and again. He liked to sit and listen to her lecture, hearing in her voice the wisdom and grace of her father.

Years later I insisted on making the daughter's final run with Árdghal. Family, friends, students, and admirers attended her deathbed. We floated in the room for days as she graciously delayed her death in favor of a few more moments to impart the wisdom she had gained. Flowers overwhelmed the home in which she lived, tokens from loved ones but also from former students and prominent public figures. Some sent them because it was a show of love and others as a show of gratitude for her life's work. An hour before her death she posed in her bed for a photograph, prominently and proudly displaying her camp tattoo, unable to resist one last opportunity to teach the world.

When the time came, her father joined us in the room. He looked at Árdghal and said, again, "Old friend." Árdghal took the clockmaker's hand and the two together embraced the daughter's spirit as it rose. To my shock, Árdghal turned to me and said, "It's time. This is your run, not mine. I am the companion here, not the presence, old friend. Send us home."

That was my hardest run. It wasn't the first time I had served as the death presence for one of my own but Árdghal was the last of the ones I looked to for guidance. A moment comes when our work finishes, not a death as much as transition. I'm not sure if we grow weary or if we are rewarded or if we simply decide it's time to release from the confines of our work with humans. Árdghal was strong and fierce and it never occurred to me that I might help him transition one day. Perhaps this is always the way with mentors. We assume that those who show us how to be brave and strong, who model for us the best of what we can be, that they will continue on forever in front of us because they are too good to do otherwise.

Now, as I watch the activity in the hospice house, I wonder what example I may be setting for those behind me. I don't share that connection between a mentor and student with any of them and that might be my biggest regret.

8 The Band Director

I manifest in the parking lot of a hospital behind a huge oak tree because the lot is full of teenagers huddled around every entrance, bench, and pickup truck in sight. Whoever this Band Director is, these kids love him. In every group I pass on my way to the door there is at least one kid bawling his eyes out while another tries to comfort him. Comforting presences are everywhere. I spot Mariah with her arms encircling a group of petite freshmen girls. She looks at me, weary, and then back at the girls.

The corridor to the elevator is no different: cheerleaders, football players in their letter jackets, and band geeks, some even clutching their instruments. Parents are sprinkled throughout the groups, doing their best to comfort, even though they too are upset. Here and there is a pastor trying to comfort people, but a few are showing signs of their own grief as they struggle to be strong for others. A whole army of comforting presences has descended on the hospital and there are at least two for every group. It's been a long time since I have felt nervous, but this scene is starting to get to me.

I make my way up the elevator and find even more people in the hall. Hospital security is doing their best to balance ministering to the community while also trying to keep a clear path down the hallway. Two students are in the room with the Band Director and his family, playing for him on their clarinet and oboe. I round the corner and suddenly realize where I am. Long ago I stopped keeping track of where I was headed when starting a run, so I didn't pay attention to the name of the city when I arrived. I spy the Coke machine in the waiting room filled with people and discover I'm back in Anne's hospital. That means I'm back in Texas where the Friday Night Lights shine bright and the halftime show is major entertainment. No wonder the place is crawling with people and presences.

I walk down the hallway to the big corner room and peer through the door. It doesn't matter that no one recognizes me. People have been coming and going for two days now and faces have become a blur for the family. The Band Director has two children, a boy and a girl in their late twenties, and both are holding vigil in their dad's room along with their mother. The younger brother notices me in the doorway. I wave, and he turns his attention back to the students playing their instruments.

The doctors found the cancer only three weeks ago, but it had already eaten up his body. It seems the Band Director had been keeping secrets about his health for years. Two days ago he had a stroke and has been unconscious ever since. I think he's waiting for the sake of his family and all of his students. He's giving them a chance to say "goodbye."

I walk back down the hallway, past all of the students, looking for a place to shed my manifest body. I pass the nurses' station and spot her. Anne has tucked herself into a small alcove in a side hallway. Her shoulders are shaking. Tianshi is hovering beside her, eyes nearly closed as she radiates her comforting presence upon Anne.

She's in great company with Tianshi. She's been around nearly as long as I have. I should continue down the hallway and get back to the task at hand.

"Excuse me, doctor, can you direct me to room 531?" It's late, I know, but I want to check on her. Anne turns and I see tears streaming down her face. "Um, what? Room 531?" She tries to gain her composure. "Sorry. Is that what you said?"

Tianshi just looks at me with utter confusion, as if to say, "What are you doing?"

"No, I mean, yes. That's the room, but I'm the one who's sorry. I didn't mean to interrupt you."

I look over her head to Tanshi's face and give her a slight shrug. Anne stares into my face for a moment and stops crying.

"Have I met you before?"

"Me? No! I mean, no. I live several hours away."

"Are you sure you haven't been here before to visit family or see a doctor?"

"I'm sure. I haven't been around here for years and years." Did I pick a manifestation that looks too much like Tiffany from last time? I have never had someone recognize me before. Never. I'm not sure what to say or even how to act.

"Sorry. My mistake then. I probably can't focus too well right now anyway. Room 531 is back down that hallway. It's the one with music coming out of it." Anne tears up again as we both hear notes floating our way from a lone saxophone.

I look down the hallway, then turn back to Anne. "My name's Sharon."

"Hi. I'm Dr. Markham."

"It's nice to meet you."

"What are you doing here? Are you a friend of Mr. O?"

I conjure a story as quickly as I can. I want to stay and talk. "I work for a music magazine now, but years ago I attended a rival school and remembered Mr. O's band. I wanted to pay my respects and maybe write a piece about him and the effect he's had on all of these kids."

"On me too. I was one of his band nerds back in the day. He taught me to love the flute and then pushed me to try the drumline." For a moment Anne smiles. She straightens up and presses down her lab coat after smoothing her hair. "Sharon, it's nice to meet you. Thanks for interrupting my little crying session, even if you didn't mean to. Somehow talking to you has helped."

"It's nice to meet you, too, Dr. Markham."

"Please, call me Anne."

"Like the mother of Mary."

Anne pauses. "Are you sure we've never met?"

"I'm sure. I don't think we would have been in high school at the same time and it's been years since I've been down this way." I feel unmoored, unsure of how to manage myself.

She turns to the counter to pick up a water bottle. Tianshi looks at me and mouths, "Go!" I quickly move back down the hallway. I find a private spot and shift. I can't believe I wasted so much time talking to her.

I spot Moébé as he drifts into the Band Director's room. I haven't been paying attention, but did they really think they needed to send another death presence? We never work in teams for runs like this, so I doubt he's here to assist.

I make my way into the room and Moébé looks at me with wide eyes and an expression that says it all. I almost missed it.

Three girls from the high school chorus have gathered at the Band Director's feet and are softly singing a hymn. The son and daughter are on either side of the Band Director and the wife is standing by his head, her hands cradling his head as if to lift it so he can hear the singing better. As the last refrain begins, I see him. The Band Director is starting to lift out of his body, but his threads don't want to release. He's not ready, but his body has betrayed him.

Moébé rises to his side and holds his hand. I hover above the daughter and take the Band Director's other hand. He doesn't want to look at us and we understand. We tell him we know; we know he's not ready and neither are his family or any of the students in the hallway, but it's time. He no longer has a choice.

He looks around the room one more time, drinking in the faces of his daughter, his son, and his wife. He never looks at us but just nods. Moébé and I get to work, trying to put him at ease and prepare him for his journey. We think he has accepted the moment but then he pulls away from us and tries to enter his body again. His spirit lies over his body but the body is finished.

The Band Director tries to fight his body and settle back in. As the body rejects the spirit, a trickle of blood drops from the body's nose. Several more comforting presences fly into the room at the moment the Band Director's wife lets out a scream. She yells for the nurses, adamant that her husband is still alive, pointing to the blood.

Anne walks in the room with two nurses and examines the body. She knows what she will find. She knows he is gone, but she goes through the motions of checking for vital signs. She knows the wife needs to see her do this. Anne turns to the wife, shaking her head. I watch as she and the nurses take the hands of the wife and begin what is often a long process. They try to explain that sometimes this happens but every time the wife wipes the Band Director's nose, more trickles out. The wife cries every time and demands that he be checked again for signs of life. The son and daughter stand in an uncomfortable sea of emotions that range from grief to shame to hope. I watch as Anne shows deep compassion and patience, pushing down the grief I know that is within her own spirit.

Moébé calls my attention back to the body and we watch as the spirit of the Band Director lifts one more time, reconciled and ashamed. We can feel his heartache as he comes to float between us, his eyes resolutely focused on the worn tile floor. He doesn't dare look at his wife or his children again. If he were still in bodily form, he would have vomited remorse all over that same floor. He knew he was sick and ignored it. In this moment he realizes things might have been different, he might not be leaving had he paid attention to the signs and taken care of himself. How many times had he thought he needed to visit the doctor then pushed the thought away, afraid of the truth?

Moébé and I wrap ourselves around him. We feel the heaviness of his soul and he needs us both to carry him onward. He realizes he made it worse by trying to go back but he couldn't help it. It wasn't fear that took him back but remorse and regret; a desire to be back just one minute more. We carry him on and he moves forward, never once looking back but keeping his gaze downward.

Moébé and I are too exhausted from the ordeal to travel but I can't collapse in the hospital. I've got to get out of here. Moébé takes my hand and we go outside. There's a nursing home next door so we collapse together as a bench under a tree. From here we can barely make out the rumble of drums. The kids in the high school drumline have heard the news and are giving their director one last roll. I can't help but think of Anne and how she said the Band Director encouraged her to play the drums as well.

Moébé starts to ask me questions but I can't talk. I can't explain what happened to me tonight or what I'm feeling. Right now, I need to just be. But I'm glad, for once, I'm not on this run alone.

9 The Funeral

Three weeks have passed since the Band Director's death, which has been just enough time for the Texas summer heat to arrive. I'm perched on top of the press box of a massive football stadium. An exception has been made and I have come on my request. Today there's no soul to transition, no run to make. I'm merely here to hold a hand.

I came early so I could watch people arrive. The Band Director was cremated, giving the school plenty of time to orchestrate a funeral suitable for honoring his legacy. The band kids are front and center and one by one they have filled the stands. Beside them are the football team and cheerleading squad. Every bleacher has four boxes of tissues strategically placed across it and I think a fourth of them must be empty already. The planners anticipated the tears but not the trash; white piles are forming under the feet of the crowd.

Parents, students, friends, fellow faculty members, and community members slowly fill the stands. Every kid has a flower in their hand, red or white for the colors of the school, in anticipation of a planned flower laying ceremony after the funeral on the 50 yard line. Every florist in Texas must have been cleared of their roses, mums, and carnations. It will take campus security hours to get the kids to leave the field later but it will be worth it.

I feel Gelion arriving behind me. I smile. Her name comes from the Greek root that means "Good news" and it suits her so well. Her gift is making death feel like good news for every one of the souls she helps transition. Maybe it's her youth but I think it's more her spirit. Was I that vibrant after only 200 years of this work? Maybe. But there's still something uniquely beautiful about Gelion. Her entire being radiates love and warm welcome.

She comes to rest beside me, settling the Band Director between us. It takes a few minutes before he can look at me. Sadness and shame are still there but I can see he's improving. This exception has been made in an effort to bring him more peace and acceptance. I nod at him and place my hand on his shoulder, then gesture to the far gates of the field.

The drumline is leading the funeral procession into the stadium and everyone is on their feet. The steady beats roll across the open field. The drum major is carrying the ashes in a box painted with the school colors. Behind her the daughter and son of the Band Director have their arms around their mother. She's standing taller than before, now carrying her sadness mixed with pride and acceptance. She wears red and white flowers on her dress, held together with a pin shaped like a treble clef.

Next comes the faculty of the high school dressed in academic regalia. They all show up in the most formal attire they can imagine, wanting in this seemingly small way to show the utmost respect to their friend and colleague. I smile as it is apparent some haven't worn such regalia in years whereas others obviously pulled them from the bag today, creases making a checkerboard pattern on the shiny polyester. Sweat drips down their faces already, but they are determined.

Finally the Band Directors from the high schools of all the surrounding counties enter, all in their own school colors but wearing black armbands on their right arm.

The last of the participants trickle in and find their seats as the marching band plays an arrangement of "Blackbird" by the Beatles. We look around the stands as an army of comforting presences take their places.

Three presences float down to the sideline where a high school junior stands shaking, trumpet in hand. I can feel his nervousness from here as he brings his instrument to his lips, letting out a brief prayer first for his success. The weighty notes of Fleetwood Mac's *Songbird* fall from his instrument then rise to meet the crowd in the stands. He performs beautifully and sets the tone for all that follows.

The Band Director takes it all in then begins to speak about the pain he's caused. All he can see are the tissues and the tears. He thinks he is to blame for the large group gathered here to mourn. He begins the litany of, "What ifs." What if he had been honest with himself about his health? What if he had gone to the doctor sooner? What if he . . . ? On and on. Gelion and I give him some time to recite his litany. It's necessary.

About five questions into his seventeen question recitation I notice a late arrival at a side gate. It's Anne, trying to slide in unnoticed but still wanting to pay her respects at the end of a long shift. I can see from here that she's exhausted but carries red and white roses in her hand.

As the Band Director finishes his process of self-blame, I point to Anne and ask him if he remembers her. He recognizes her from the hospital and starts to question why she's here but then assumes she's here out of some work obligation. He thinks she feels that she should be present and counted as a member of the community and no more. He doesn't recognize her.

I share with him what Anne told me in the hospital; how she had been one of his students and he had pushed her to take up the drums after first teaching her the flute. He looks at me, then at her, and recognition dawns on his face. Then I watch as he slowly moves his head to take in every face in the crowd that has gathered. He stops making his own list and starts to listen. The speakers number the ways he affected their lives; it goes far beyond teaching them how to play their first three notes or how to march and play without tripping or bumping into each other. With every word and every face he begins to heal. The shame inside him begins to transform into satisfaction and reconciliation. The satisfaction turns to pride as his daughter and son come forward to speak. He looks from them to his wife and back again. Then to every past and present student that he worked with who sits in the crowd. They are all his children in one way or another.

The son finishes his eulogy and the band stands. They move to take the field for one last tribute. The Band Director lifts with them and we think he's simply moving with the students but then he starts to float further away. Gelion smiles and starts to go with him but stops. This time he's ready and makes the run on his own. He doesn't need us to pull him, nor does he need to stay to watch the rest of the funeral. The healing that remains is for the living now, not for him.

10 The Village

Nearly a hundred of us are gathered on a large stone formation outside the village. Moébé and I sit near each other and look at the scene in front of us. Among the rubble and barely-there homes are hundreds of comforting presences, one for each human.

I despise being back here. All of us have made runs to collect souls from this place over the past few years. The human Bible speaks of famine, pestilence, and war. This village and others across Syria have been experiencing all three. The souls rise from this place almost daily. If it's not a lack of food, then it's a lack of medicine. If it's not a lack of medicine, it's a lack of water. . . that is, if the drones and airstrikes haven't already killed them.

This many of us gathered together can mean only one thing: a potential strike. I hate waiting for war. Waiting for death is part of the process and we've all learned to pass the time one way or another. Generally, it's a pleasant time when loved ones come to the person to say "Goodbye," or "I'm sorry." As with the Landowner, sometimes the waiting is filled with blessing and beauty as the soul dances in and out of the body.

Not here. Not in war. We wait to see how stupid and cruel humans can be to one another. We wait to see if the humans in control will recognize the men, women, and children in the valley before us as fellow human beings or simply as "collateral damage"; isn't that what humans call it? "Collateral damage" means "you're only a number." In my nearly eight hundred years as a death presence it hasn't changed, none of it. The weapons have "advanced," as the humans like to say, but all that means is that more of us are needed to respond to their wars and violence.

Lòng Hăng Hái settles next to me. "At it again, I see." She's been a presence nearly as long as I have.

"I hate being back here."

"Me, too. I was here yesterday for an infant. The mother couldn't produce enough milk for it. You see Griffin in the valley? That's the house. I can hear the mother crying."

I look at the village and spot Griffin hovering in a home riddled with bullet holes. The light pours into the house through a large hole in one of the walls, likely made by shrapnel from another strike. The mother and father are in there with their remaining child.

"They're refugees, aren't they?" I ask as I turn to Hái.

"Yes. They fled here from two villages over. They arrived four days ago. They had just found this abandoned house when the infant died." She turns to me. "What is troubling you? Moébé is irritable and will not tell me what happened, only that something is wrong. Tell me."

I look back over the village, then down to the ground. "I know her name."

"What?"

"I know her name," I repeat.

"Whose name? I do not understand. I need more."

"Lately I have seen the same doctor again and again on different runs. I never have paid attention to those around our spirits, only enough to get a feel for the situation and how they might be feeling. Those around our spirits are the work for the others, not for me. But this one, this doctor. . . I don't know. I keep being pulled into conversation with her and I don't know why. It is distracting and unnerving and not what I am meant to do. Tending to doctors and nurses, family and friends, that's not my job."

Then I wait for Hái's judgment. Instead, she allows the silence to hang between us among the horrible waiting.

She looks at me, then up, then back to the terrified villagers in the valley. "All of these years I've wondered how you could do it; how you could stay so detached from the living souls in the room and singularly focused on the dying. I've admired you for it, even, for a time. But now, I'm not so sure."

I look at her, a little hurt and more confused. "It's the job! It's what we do!"

"No, Phe, it's what you do. Most of us gave up a long time ago on trying to stay separated. The mother down there," she nods to the village, "her name is Laila. The father? He's Houmam. Sara is the big sister. She's the last one of six children and the oldest. She held each of her smaller siblings with their mother and watched them die."

I stare at Hái in utter amazement and heartbreak. It's my turn to let the silence hover.

I start to say something when we all spot it—the light on the bottom of the drone. I want something different for Laila and

Houmam and Sara. I want the drone to be smaller, armed with cameras rather than bombs. But I know better; we all know better. In dismay we prepare ourselves for our flight down to the village as we watch the comforting presences. They have stopped moving and have grabbed the shoulders of the humans in front of them, bowing their heads.

11 Oxygen Man, Carl

We don't tire but we do get exhausted. I railed against the men who ordered the drone strike on Sara's village, for their callousness and inhumanity. How could the villagers be nothing more than collateral damage to anyone? How could they only be part of equations, game plans for the gods of war? But the truth strikes to my core: I've done the same. I hide behind the Band Director, the Landowner, the Tourist, and the others. These titles form the wall separating me from the humans, keeping me distanced from the daughters, sons, wives, and husbands—those left for the comforting presences. They have been types, humans, rather than people with names. I like it that way. And I like it that way still. But what does that make me?

Those of us on the village run were given less catastrophic runs this round. Transitioning so many souls at one time takes a greater toll on us than assisting one at a time. I'm hanging out in a hospital cafeteria in Little Rock. Oxygen man is sitting at the table next to me. He's here for chemo for the cancer in his lungs, a cancer that will likely kill him later this year. What the doctors haven't seen is the aneurysm in his brain. That's why I'm here. He's nervous about the chemo, worried about his wife; he has a second mortgage on their home that she doesn't know about, one that his life insurance policy won't cover. His blood pressure is through the roof but the doctors haven't realized it yet. He's a time bomb and I'm here to see if they change his blood pressure meds before the aneurysm blows.

Carl, his name is Carl. His wife is Janice. They've been married thirty-seven years and love their dachshunds like the children they couldn't have. I've been replaying my conversation with Hái and have promised myself to make more of an effort or, at least, to pay closer attention. I take my first steps of vulnerability, opening myself to learn a little something about this couple.

When Janice suggested they go to the cafeteria for lunch, I thought it was a great idea. It meant I could manifest and sit with a newspaper and a Coke. I was grateful when Carl agreed and slowly reached for his IV pole to use as a walker. He's not fast on his feet, giving me plenty of time to wait behind in his room and manifest before following them downstairs. They went through the line and Carl picked up some Jell-O and Sprite to ease his nausea. I settled at a table near them, having taken the form of a doctor. It's given me plenty of time to sit and listen to their conversation as well as their silences. I like Carl and Janice. They're here for a terrible reason, but they're making the most of their time together.

I get up to refill my drink. It's early summer in Little Rock and the cold Coke tastes even better than usual. I grab a magazine left behind on another table and return to my seat. I'm scanning the pictures when I hear, "Hello!"

It's Anne. How can it be Anne? This is Arkansas, not Texas.

"Hi?" I have no idea what to do.

"Sorry, don't I know you? I thought I recognized you but now I'm not so sure. Have you ever done a rotation in Texas? Or maybe it's Chicago. Did you do your residency in Chicago?"

What is she talking about? I look down and remember—the lab coat. Why did I manifest as a doctor?

"No. Sorry. I've never been to Texas (liar) and I did all of my training in California (yeah, right). Sorry to disappoint." I'm being rude. I know it. I have never had a human recognize me in a manifest form, much less approach me. I'm pretty good at blending in and just becoming part of the woodwork.

"Are you sure? I mean, I know you're sure about where you've been and trained, but are you sure we don't know each other? I swear I've seen you before." That's when it hits me: she's a seer. I've never met one because they are so rare. It's probably why she's a great doctor and why her patients love her as much as they do. It's also why she cries every time one of her patients dies. Her capacity for empathy is beyond any human measure. She's touched, probably a comforting presence in the making, and she sees me, really sees me, but she doesn't know that's what she's doing. I have no clue how to handle this.

"You know, you look a little familiar, too. Maybe we've attended a conference together or something." What am I doing? I should be moving away from an interaction like this. My entire existence I have stayed away from humans unless they were near death and it was on a run. I'm beginning to doubt myself, my dedication to keeping my distance and doing my job. But I want to talk. I want to know more and have a "normal" conversation, even if it is just to see what it feels like.

She smiles, "Maybe that's it. Do you mind if I sit down?"

"Please." I'm in a hospital cafeteria and a very healthy human wants to sit and visit. I feel the eyes of every comforting presence in the room turn to my table and burn through my back. For a moment they forget the families in the room and linger in shock. I want to float up, turn around, and yell at them, "I know! I have no idea what's happening either!" They sense my unease and turn back to their work.

Anne sits down. "Thanks," she says, "I'm new and haven't met many people. Actually, I don't even know where the doctors' lounge is yet. I was so glad, and surprised, to see another doctor here."

Never again. Never again will I manifest in a white lab coat. Never. "I'm Anne. I've been working in Texas, but a friend recommended I try traveling work for a while after a particularly difficult case. I was a little too emotionally close to one of my patients who died."

"Hi. I'm. . .Sam. It's short for Samantha."

She looks me square in the face for a moment then says, "Huh. I wouldn't guess you for a Samantha. It's a great name, it just doesn't seem to suit you."

I laugh.

"Sorry!" she blurts out, "I don't mean to be rude. Sometimes things just tumble out of me without my even knowing where they come from. I promise I don't mean to offend."

"No offense taken, I assure you."

We make small talk; isn't that what humans call it? I have never had to do this before. Usually I interact with humans who are emotionally exhausted and can manage only minimal chatter. They forget me soon enough and let me recede to the background. Not Anne. Her focus is squarely on me and her energy pours out of her in a thousand little questions and stories.

"Anyway, 'Anne' isn't my real name either. At least, it's not my birth name. My birth certificate says 'Patrice.' It was my grandmother's name, but when I made my first communion I fell in love with 'Anne.' I'm intrigued by the idea that Jesus had a grandmother. My grandmothers were both amazing women and I'd like to think Jesus had that in his life as well."

"Oh, he had them in spades, believe me." Anne starts to take a sip of coffee but stops the cup midair to stare at me. I want to tell her all about Anne, mother of Mary. I want to tell her about how lovingly Anne held Jesus when Mary returned from Bethlehem. Like the Anne in front of me, the grandmother of Jesus has an immeasurable capacity for empathy still today. I want to tell this Anne that her namesake worried for Joseph and Mary as they travelled for the census. Watching Joseph and Mary leave the city when Mary was well into her third term was one of the hardest things Anne ever had to do. She's one of the inspirations for the comforting presences as they care for humans the world over.

"What's your name? Your real name?" I can't tell if she's being funny (human jokes are lost on me) or serious. Her eyes tell me she's being serious.

"Sam. That really is my name."

"That may be on your birth certificate but I get the feeling you're someone else. What do you call yourself?" I hesitate. I can feel the comforting presences around me grow uneasy. I take a deep breath and look at her.

"Phe. My name is Phe."

At that moment, Oxygen Man, Carl, passes out and slumps to the ground. Don't worry, it's not the aneurysm. His blood pressure dropped. It will be the sign the doctors need to put him on medication and prevent his aneurysm from blowing.

Anne jumps up and rushes over to care for him, giving me the perfect opportunity to escape. I dart into the bathroom, drop the lab coat and disappear.

12 Chu Qing, the Virus Outbreak Patient

I find myself on the other side of the world for this run. It's been a long time since I've been assigned to Asia and this time I'm waiting in a hospital in Wuhan, China. I thought I might be called here soon. I've been hearing from friends that our kind have been called here with increasing frequency.

Sabine is hovering near the doctor tending the patient in the bed next to mine. I can tell by the look on her face that this isn't good. I also know that however long this outbreak lasts, Sabine will stay, just as she did during the Black Death years ago, caring for the staff as they desperately try to save others.

Malak hovers beside her. He's here for the patient, waiting for the doctor's efforts to fail. Malak and I have known each other for centuries. He was a newer presence in the middle ages when the plague first showed itself. I remember being impressed by how quickly and earnestly he learned this work. He exudes both confidence and tenderness. All spirits feel immediately safe when they see him.

Whatever this is, it appears to be spreading fast and reminds me of previous pandemics, though this hasn't been called that yet by human authorities. It is isolated to this region of China but all available beds have been moved into this ward and I can see through the window a frantic effort to add more temporary bed space. There is a large construction crew working with heavy equipment to add temporary wards on to the hospital.

All we can hear is the labored breathing all around us and the hurried clicking of feet on tile as the healthcare professionals race around us from bed to bed. A legion of comforting presences swarm around them, their serene faces not betraying the chaos that surrounds us.

There are no family members or friends here for our comforting presences to tend to, unless they are in neighboring beds being watched by one of my kind. The healthcare authorities have learned enough to know how contagious this is, having seen entire families brought low by this virus. I can see among the comforting presences there are a few death presences trailing the doctors and nurses as well. I wonder how many of the healthcare workers know they are sick and dying but are too committed to their patients to stop. I have seen this special kind of bravery and determination in many sick wards over time.

I turn my attention to my own charge, Chu Qing. Her husband brought her here a few days ago. His own breathing was labored but he was so concerned for her that he didn't notice. He died this morning and she will soon follow. Their daughter lives in Shenzhen and only knows that her parents felt they were coming down with a cold four days ago. She's heard something is sweeping over Wuhan but not that her parents have and will succumb to the new virus. Some of our comforting presences will tend to her while she waits for a phone call, expecting one from a parent but receiving one instead from a hospital agent.

Outbreaks present a special emotional challenge for humans. The mass death of war can be blamed on a perceived evil adversary. With war there is always a "them" to rail against, someone to throw their anger towards. I have found that humans crave blame in the presence of death. They need someone to be responsible, someone to fight against in a hunger for justice and balance, someone to arrest and crucify to feed their anger at a world turned upside down.

But viruses and bacteria give humans no opportunity for blame. They simply develop and infect, then mutate and spread further. My personal theory is that they are Earth's immune response. Whenever she, the Earth, recognizes a threat to her delicate balance, she mounts a response just as the cells of my charge, Chu Qing, have been mounting a response to this virus. If Earth perceives humans as a threat, like a parasite or infection, she activates her immune system by creating soldiers to fight off her perceived invaders. She guards her balance. She was created with it and she will do what it takes to maintain it.

That's my theory, anyway, but it would be of little comfort to the woman in the bed before me. All Chu Qing knows is that she is suffering and wants relief.

If this virus spreads to the rest of the world as quickly as it is doing here, we will have another global pandemic. It doesn't take much imagination for me to know how humanity will respond. In the absence of a true foe, they will manufacture one, if not many. Scapegoats will be named and persecuted and they will rail against one another, working hard to manufacture a "them" in the absence of one. Blame is too valuable to humans for them to leave it alone. And their egos are too fragile for them to accept any personal responsibility for how their actions might be leading the Earth to launch an attack on them. Blame is a ready distraction and can easily be manufactured in times of hysteria.

Just as before, different people or peoples will be targeted in different parts of the world. Everyone will be wrong but that won't matter because pointing a finger and creating a false enemy is more important to them than justice. There will be investigations, lawsuits, crimes born of hate and discrimination, and plenty of fear to go around.

But it won't stop the intense and persistent pain of sudden loss. Humans will wonder why they don't feel better after finding a target at which to direct their blame, fear and hatred. They won't understand why everything isn't "normal" after all of their arguing and fighting. Meanwhile, millions will die and mourning will be delayed or denied rather than managed and nurtured. Humans do not handle feelings of helplessness well.

I look up to see twenty more patients brought in just as eight current ones are lifting from their bodies. Among them is Malak's charge. I watch with wonder as he embraces the woman's spirit and eases her confusion, even as he is ushering her on. All the while, a nurse has confirmed that the woman is dead and already is moving her body in order to bring another patient to fill the bed. Sabine is there with the nurse, hand on her shoulder.

Chu Qing's lungs begin to gurgle and rattle and I know she will be among the next to die. I see Malak drift over to one of the newly accepted patients, not pausing from his work to rest or recover. I turn to Chu Qing and watch as her breathing stops and her spirit lifts. It is my turn to catch and comfort, then send her on, before joining Malak for the next round.

13 Langston, the Infant

The emergency room lights burn down on the orderly as he resets the room for the next patient. This space can't wait for the recovery after death. There are twenty people in the waiting room, most of them with the stomach virus going around, and the staff needs the bed. It's built for a large adult but only five minutes ago held the body of an infant, Langston.

I arrived mid-morning to the same house I had visited only four months ago. Although birth in the twenty-first century is much safer than it was even forty years ago, we still attend every one. The difference between birth and death is but a breath, and we watch each soul come into the world, hoping we won't be needed for either the infant or the mother. In days past we would watch the same midwife work every birth and death in an area until births were moved almost exclusively to hospitals and undertakers became more common. Midwives only work births now, but we're still present at both.

I didn't pay attention to this infant's name at his birth but now I made a note of it. I noticed the big black and white letters above his crib, proudly hung on the blue walls: "LANGSTON," named for famed poet Langston Hughes. The infant's mother is a high school English teacher in the Baltimore City School System. Every year she makes sure her students know that Hughes was mostly raised by his grandmother, like so many of them. Under the sign in the nursery, she painted on the wall, "Hold fast to dreams for if dreams die life is a broken-winged bird that cannot fly"—from Hughes's famous poem, "Dreams."

I looked into the crib to see the infant Langston asleep, his breathing growing more and more shallow. In a matter of minutes the breaths faded into nothing and Langston floated just above his body. I pulled him to me, cradling him in my arms. His eyes brightened as recognition crossed his face.

Infant deaths are the most beautiful and the most wretched for me. We make the runs for the infants whose births we attend because they recognize us. Their memories of our realm haven't fully disappeared, so they look up at us with the same knowing eyes in their deaths as they did just before their births. The delicate silver threads that connect their souls to their bodies whisper as they separate. There is no pain nor fear for them, only peace.

But the pain for the families is a different story. Once Langston was on his way into the dimension of the dead, I collapsed in the corner of his crib as a baby blanket and waited for the sitter, his eleven-year-old cousin from next door. She came into the room ten minutes later to check on her "Sweet Cuz," as she called him. The school teacher mother, Kayla, was on summer break and had stepped out for an hour to go to the gym. Langston's big cousin did exactly as she was told and put the baby to bed. There is nothing she could have done differently to save Langston, but she will never be able to accept that fact. Her entire life she'll question every second of that morning, begging to go back in time and do something, anything, differently.

From the corner of the crib I watched the cousin's confusion and fear turn to action as she called 911 and then her own mother, who was at work but rushed to the hospital to meet the ambulance when it arrived. The paramedics did the best they could for Langston's tiny body. They grabbed me to wrap him in when they took him down to the ambulance. They saw his blue lips and knew he was gone but still tried their hardest to make the impossible happen. Mariah arrived to hold vigil over the little cousin and a team of comforting presences met us at the hospital for the rest of the family as well as the hospital staff.

People think the doctors, nurses, EMTs, and support staff experience death as just another tragic day in the emergency room, but it's not true. They mourn every death and question whether or not they did their best to save the person. An infant death is ten times harder on everyone. No one wants to go home with the memory of watching a fifteen pound body being taken to the morgue.

Even the orderly is taking more time than usual to clean the room. He yearns for his mop strokes to wipe out the pain in the hospital from this death. He lifts them as prayers in what amounts to a litany for Langston and his suffering family. Past him I can see through the walls to the consultation room on the other side of the ER where the mother has crumpled to the floor. The chaplain is on the floor next to her, the chaplain's hand on the mother's shoulder. He's doing his best just to be present for her in her inconsolable pain.

I hear a police officer in the hallway talking to a social worker. They are clear this is a case of SIDS but want to help the mother track down her husband. He's a journalist embedded with the US Army and left two weeks ago on a three week assignment. It could take days to reach him, if they can connect the dots enough to figure out who to contact to start that process.

In the meantime, Kayla screams out her pain for her Langston, now lost to my world.

I fade away and disappear while the orderly takes out the trash, his last duty before opening the room up for the next patient, the next family. I leave with a sharp awareness of how exhausted I have become.

I want to lie to myself and say that one soul blends into another, each death fades into the next in the river of my work. I want to believe that I haven't noticed the passage of human time and the effect their "advances" have had on my existence. But the truth is that I remember every one, every run I've made in over seven and a half centuries. I know their faces and the color and shape their threads took as they let go of their bodies. In my mind's eye I can see the emotion each of those persons experienced at the moment of their death and how it changed as they prepared to move on. All of them are there in my memory like a portfolio of my work that follows me on every new run, waiting for the next addition.

14 Mariapia, the COVID patient

The world is desperately trying to catch up with the reality of this pandemic. Much of the world assumed, or hoped it would stay in China, but the virus replicates so quickly and goes undetected in so many that it will cover the Earth. For older humans, like Mariapia, they will barely have time to know they have been infected before they die. I arrived in Modena seven hours ago and Mariapia will die before nightfall tomorrow.

She has been placed in one of the newest beds added to the intensive care unit specifically for COVID patients. Respirators gurgle and hiss all around us as alarms keep sounding to alert the healthcare team of dropping pulse rates, blood pressure, and oxygen levels. The doctors and nurses can't respond to the alarms quickly enough to provide anyone in the unit with even thirty seconds of quiet.

Somewhere in the parking lot, one of our comforting presences has found Mariapia's son. Luca is wracked with guilt. He travelled to Milan on business, thinking he could escape the fast-spreading virus if he entered and exited the city quickly enough. He didn't know one of his colleagues had travelled to China and that the virus was silently circulating among their team. It was over a week before one of them fell ill and sparked the rest of the team to be tested. Two days before he learned he should be tested, Luca visited his mother.

The moment Luca received his positive results, he raced to his mother's house. He intended to speak with her through an open window to warn her. He didn't want to say it over the phone. He knocked on her door but she didn't appear. He yelled her name but she didn't answer. He pounded but there was no response. He found his key to her home and opened the door to find her collapsed on the floor near the phone. I was there beside her already. She had lost consciousness only two hours before he arrived.

Luca called for the ambulance and held his mother. The emergency response team made him isolate himself in her bedroom before they would enter the residence. He watched from her doorway as they shifted her to the stretcher and carried her off. He didn't understand yet that he would never see her again.

I'll be here for Mariapia as she passes. She'll be more worried about Luca than she will be upset at her death. She had been following the news and had a premonition that she would be in the first wave to die; she just didn't know how she would contract the disease.

As I watch her spirit rise from her body, she looks at me and registers understanding. Her eyes grow wide and she knows it was Luca. She falls into my arms and would have wept if spirits had that ability. She knows the guilt will be unbearable for him. He has been a faithful son and he loves his mother dearly. This will crush him.

I assure her that he will be well and that he is in good hands with our comforting presences. But I don't know this. I have seen guilt bring slow spiritual death and sometimes physical death to too many for me to tell her this with any real confidence. The truth is that the guilt will be magnified by the fact that he couldn't be by her side as she died. He would have been with her every moment, never leaving her side, had she died in a different time from a different cause. Perhaps he would have been with her in her own home. At least, that is how he always had imagined it. He wanted to be with his mother as she died as a way of showing gratitude for her being the one who brought him life.

Mariapia holds onto me for a long time, not ready to move. I hold her and she doesn't notice that the medical team has rushed into the room to try to save her. She doesn't feel the shock of the paddles or even appear to have heard the hum of the charge or the crack as the electricity entered her body. All she can see in her mind is Luca.

I try to reassure her but there is little I can do. I hope she'll have time later to visit Luca in whatever way possible to see how he is. Or maybe not. It will depend on too many things for me to see clearly at this time.

Mariapia pulls back and looks at me. She touches my face as she studies it. She instinctively has a mother's touch, even in death. I feel the tenderness in her fingers and the deep love of her heart. It is beautiful despite our horrific surroundings. She turns and we continue with her transition.

I collapse in the parking lot as a discarded cup. I want to see what happens with Luca. A comforting presence is in the car with him as he receives the call from the hospital. The sobs gush out of him, then turn to a hacking cough. The hospital worker on the phone hears and asks him where he is. Within minutes a healthcare team rushes out and takes him inside.

I transition and follow them. I haven't been called up for a run and I have a feeling about this. They take Luca to their triage area for suspected COVID patients and he tells them of his positive test results. I feel the exasperation surge inside the nurses caring for him. They move him immediately to the COVID wing, not far from where his mother had been.

I don't leave. There's no point. I let it be known that I'll take this run and wait. Luca won't live more than 48 hours. It is hard for me to tell if it is the heartbreak or the virus that kills him. It doesn't really matter.

When it's time, Mariapia is right beside me. She reaches for her son's hand when she knows he has only a few breaths left. He senses her and tightens his fist. I'm not sure if he'll be ashamed or happy to see her, but I'm certain they both will know they are loved.

15 Adalberto

Death by suicide due to depression is always complicated. Of all the forms death takes, it is the least predictable. Souls that separate by the will of their own person can be complicated or chaotic, furious or ecstatic, remorseful or relieved. I never know until they fully separate and then look at me. Even their separation from the body takes different forms.

I hesitate to talk about this one. Humans don't know what to do with depression and certainly do worse when it leads to death by suicide. Of all the deaths, they fear it the most. The mere word sends them into an internal state of panic. They don't want to connect with it or, more honestly, don't want to admit that they do. Death demands a compassionate response but compassion in turn demands emotional engagement, and few are willing to engage emotionally with suicide. Either they don't want to attempt to imagine the complex emotions that lead to taking one's own life or they don't want to admit that they don't need to imagine them because they have felt them closely and often. It's the death most riddled with shame.

This suicide was of the particularly heartbreaking variety for me so I've crumpled in the hotel room as a napkin on a room-service tray. Last night Adalberto ordered his favorite foods, five meals worth of steak, lobster, dessert and bread. On the tray I blend in with the rest of the leftovers from his last meal.

This could be any hotel room in any city for any business traveler. It is both comfortable and "well appointed" while simultaneously feeling sterile, standard, and sad. It is utilitarian yet with a desperate veneer of hospitality. This room happens to be in Rio de Janeiro and happens to have been the last place Adalberto breathed life.

I learned before moving him along that tomorrow his company will discover he has been embezzling money from them for years. This will lead to his wife's finding out that the money he pocketed went to provide a very comfortable life for his mistress of 14 years, which in turn will lead to his children's learning they have three half siblings. Within 72 hours he will have shattered the lives of all of those he loves most in the world.

Sitting and waiting for souls separated by self-inflicted death is excruciating. We can't interfere with the processes of humanity. It's not that it's not allowed, it's that God created us specifically without the capability to do so. Our purpose is to be present and catch the spirits when they lift, jolt, fly, tear, or otherwise separate from their physical plane.

People who travel for business these days carry with them plenty of drugs; some for sleeping, some for waking, some for jet lag, some for blood pressure. As the 21st century has developed, business travelers have become walking medicine cabinets.

Adalberto was no exception; he decided to take them all. He was an avid weightlifter and added into his cocktail his pre-workout pills as well as performance enhancers. His heart didn't stand a chance. I waited as his body violently rebelled against the drugs then succumbed to them. When his spirit lifted, his body was wrecked and exhausted. He looked at me for a moment and said, "I'm ready. Whatever the devil has waiting, I deserve it."

That's when I realized it would be the most difficult sort of suicide for me.

I looked at him and said, "it doesn't work like that."

The conversation played out as it all too often does in these cases. He was confused and angry, demanding to go to hell because he deserved it. That's when I learned of his situation and the reasons he took his own life. I also quickly realized he had been formed by one of the religious traditions that teaches that death by one's own hands is a direct path to hell and damnation.

Adalberto wanted me to tell him he was going to hell. He wanted me to tell him God judged him harshly and had tremendous punishment waiting for him. He felt a need to go to this place of humanity's worst imaginings because he knew he deserved it. He had punished himself out of a desire for the punishment to continue well into eternity.

I've repeated this exchange with humans countless times, each bringing me heartbreak and pain at realizing just how little they accept about the nature of God. Maybe it's that they don't understand, but I think it's that they don't want to. They don't want a God who loves unconditionally. They don't want to know they are loved and forgiven and accepted. Actually, I had to learn the word "forgiveness" in my training because we spirits don't have this concept. Unconditional love renders such a concept unnecessary. We speak of "reconciliation" instead because the action always is on the part of the one who has turned away from God and not on God herself. She exists as pure unbounded and all-encompassing love. She only ever is waiting for her creation to come home. All they need to do is fully embrace who they are as beloved and how they belong to the whole of God's beloved creation. Forgiveness implies being shut out of love and a need to be restored or brought back in. With God, this is never the case. There are no doors, no boundaries, no possibilities of closing.

Adalberto was the most difficult of sorts because he argued with me. His spirit was all anger and rage and shame. He wanted hell, said he needed it. He tried to refuse to move forward with me unless I told him seas of fire and torment awaited him. There's nothing I can do in these cases. Their guilt and shame are too strong, too deeply rooted. All I can do is push them forward, knowing that they will comprehend and heal once they become a part of the next.

But it leaves me exhausted and confused. I know of God's love and her loving nature not by faith but by experience. I was born of it. It's all I've ever known. Yet again and again I have to struggle with humans who refuse it. I have to watch as they reject it while God continues to pour it out from her being. My peace comes from knowing that Adalberto will be embraced, restored, and healed. Over time, he will know peace and will let go of the shame and blame that threw him into despair.

16 Annette

Even in a pandemic deaths of the regular sort continue, but they easily become lost. Those who mourn the regular losses of life in times like these usually don't understand why they feel neglected or invisible. Subconsciously they come to feel their loss isn't as important because it isn't related to the wider crisis gripping the world.

I watch Annette putter around her New York City studio apartment. In a different time I would have manifested as a familiar face earlier in the week waiting in line behind her at the corner bodega. I would have spun some story about being new to the city and asked her for her neighborhood recommendations. Maybe we would have stepped outside together to look down 9th Ave long enough for her to point out her favorite diner. She would have recommended the matzo ball soup but not the pastitsio.

But these are COVID times and the city is shut down. I know pandemics well enough by now to understand what's coming. The rest of the world watched China and Italy and now watches NYC, no longer wondering if the virus will reach them but when, how quickly, and how severely. When Annette sees me in a few short minutes, I won't be familiar to her but a shock.

I find myself mourning this lost opportunity. It would have been nice to hear her describe the matzo ball soup she orders from the Jewish deli around the corner or how she prefers the silkiness of the bechamel sauce in the pastitsio from the Greek diner six blocks away. I'll never know these tastes but I imagine Annette's description would have been vivid enough to make me think one day I might. Right now she's microwaving canned pasta and I can feel her sadness and longing for something else, something fresh. Her life disappeared when the lockdown began. She lives alone and, as a compassionate and warm-hearted extrovert, her community on the streets and in the shops is everything for her. Not being around her usual people has been a heavy weight to bear. She can go days now without hearing her own voice.

Depression and loneliness hang over the city. I watch out the window as comforting presences fly between the tall buildings, rushing to their next spirit who feels the most need. I sense nervousness and uncertainty in the new ones. God has created and commissioned more to address the need of such times, much the same as she did during the Black Death and this world's great wars.

Annette is distracted by her thoughts and doesn't use a cloth to pull the bowl out of the microwave. It takes a moment for her brain to register the extreme heat because it has been numbed by her thoughts of all she is missing by being stuck at home. She yelps and the bowl crashes to the floor, breaking as it flings bright red tomato sauce across the cabinet doors. She turns to the sink to run cool water on her hand. As the burn starts to cool she feels weakness in one side of her body. She mutters aloud to herself and realizes her voice sounds funny. It is then that she slumps to the floor, one hand falling on her chest and the other coming to rest among the pasta.

I hover near her, placing my hand on her own, the one on her chest. She looks at me. Her spirit hasn't released. It will take over an hour for the stroke to stop her body from working completely. I find myself talking to her, explaining what's happening and that she's not alone. This pandemic is changing me and my heart breaks for how distanced everyone is from one another, how humans are yearning for physical touch and companionship. She looks in my eyes afraid but with a fear that gradually softens into acceptance. Annette trusts me.

Hái's words from the attack on the Syrian village come back to me. As I look in Annette's eyes, I realize I trust her too. I trust that she will listen to me and accept what I have come to do. I trust that she will accept me. We look at each other for the length of time it takes her body to give up and her spirit to lift and pull away from it.

As her spirit severs the last thread, she turns to me and says, "Thank you. I feared I would be alone and because of you I wasn't. Death was still painful but your eyes told me it would all be well. Thank you."

All I manage to say in return is, "Thank you," before sending her spirit on.

I rest in the kitchen alone in my true form. I am safe here to be myself and think. For a whole week, no one will know that Annette has died. It will take that long for her great nephew to call and then worry enough to send the police. If there wasn't a shutdown, she would have been found by noon tomorrow. The bodega owner would have realized she failed to come for her daily breakfast sandwich and coffee, along with her racing tips and news. Annette was an avid gambler on the horses, and the bodega owner stayed up on racing news just to be able to talk to her, seeing her smile and feeling her enthusiasm. But the bodega is closed and there's no one to miss her.

Suddenly I feel overwhelmed by sadness. Annette is real for me, not just one more job completed but a spirit I wish I had known more. I'm unsure of myself these days. Am I exhausted and weary? Or am I evolving and gaining wisdom?

17 Michael

I start lifting from the floor of Annette's apartment without realizing it. Conditions must have gotten worse and I'm being sent on a run without even knowing it. I'm not ready to leave. I want to hold Annette's empty hand and watch over her bodily shell, at least a little longer. But I have no choice. Even as I reach for her I find myself flying out the window and uptown.

I soar past and alongside thousands of presences. The comforting and death presences both move in and out of every building. This is an urgent era and there's no time for stopping. I spot the hospital in front of me and know that's my destination. I quickly find myself in the COVID unit and settling above a man in his fifties who otherwise looks to be in excellent health.

I spot Gelion attending a spirit a few beds over and begin to ask about mine, but she looks at the door, then at me. To my surprise, Anne walks into the room, fully covered in protective clothing and wearing a respirator. I can see her spirit well through all the protective layers and sense how exhausted and worried she is. I start to say something to her but then realize I'm in my natural form and not a manifest one.

She walks towards me and for a moment I think she can see me. I'm sure she's looking directly at me but her eyes peer through me at the man in the bed. She takes his hand and checks his vitals, studying the machines above his head. As I watch her I open myself to understand who this man is.

Michael. His life plays through my consciousness and my heart sinks. He is a doctor who has been caring for COVID patients since the virus first attacked the city. He has cared for countless patients, even as he had little understanding of what was happening to them. The symptoms of this disease are ever changing and it has been difficult for him and the other doctors and nurses to keep up. Two days ago he knew he had contracted it and his body was too tired to fight it. As Anne touches his hand I see his spirit lift, and I know then that he is aware of what is going to happen to him.

Anne checks his vitals one more time before squeezing his hand and walking out of the room. I see Michael's threads are still strong enough to buy me some time and decide to fly behind her. She escapes into a stairwell and sits down, pulling off her hood and respirator mask. I fly further up the steps and manifest as a nurse in scrubs, two Coca-colas in hand. I walk down the stairs and act surprised to find her on the stairs.

"Oh! Sorry. I didn't mean to interrupt you, but are you okay?"

Anne sniffles and wipes her nose on her sleeve before looking up. Her eyes are red and wet but few tears have escaped. She's been too busy to drink and her body has no tears to give. She says nothing.

"Sorry. Stupid question I know. I was on my way to take this to a friend but you look like you could use it more." I reach out my hand

and she accepts one of the Cokes hesitantly. I let go of the can then step back at least six feet.

I lean quietly on the stair rail and watch as she opens the can, hearing the familiar hiss before she takes her first sips. She breathes deeply between tastes of the cold sweetness and I hold the silence for her.

"You know, when I came to help with this damned disease I never imagined I would be taking care of colleagues." Anne sucks in more air for a sob that will yield no tears.

"If you don't mind me asking, why are you here? Or maybe how?"

I watch her rub her face hard and press down on her eyes before focusing on me for the first time, a flash of recognition sparking in her eyes. She decides, before speaking, she must know me from around the hospital. "I have no family so I work temporary placements around the country. When I heard the virus had spread to New York, my former placement released me from my contract so I could respond and come immediately."

"But why? Most people are praying the virus doesn't spread to their hospital, but you've intentionally placed yourself in the middle of this mess. Why?" I try not to sound pushy or nosy but I'm genuinely interested.

"My grandfather died of COPD. I took a break from working to become his main caregiver. He and I were the only two left in the family and he was my anchor. I moved in with him and listened as his lungs became weaker and weaker." She looks at me squarely with the force of someone who no longer theorizes about death but knows it fully and brutally. “I know what it looks like for a body to crave oxygen and not be able to have it, no matter how hard it grasps for it.”

I don’t ask again but I still struggle to understand. For most humans, an experience as she had with her grandfather would drive them away from witnessing anything similar. For most humans, trauma drives them away from any event that might trigger them or, worse, re-traumatize them.

“I’m sorry; do I know you from the COVID ward? Are you a nurse there? I know you.” Anne studies my face, then settles her gaze on my eyes. I realize I’ve been staring at her.

“No. I work the orthopedic wing, but I’m sure we’ve bumped into each other in the cafeteria. Speaking of which, I should go back to the vending machines and get another Coke for the person that one was intended for.”

Anne looks at the Coke next to her and smiles. “Tell your friend, ‘thanks’ for unknowingly sharing her drink with me.”

I smile back and nod before bounding up the stairs and slipping back into my natural form. I see Michael’s body struggling and come to float beside him. Gelion looks at me and I expect to find judgment but instead she merely looks at me while projecting a knowing energy of comfort my way. I am afraid I haven’t seen her as well as I should have either. I’ve missed a millennium of knowing the spirits I have helped, and now I suspect that I have failed to fully know my fellow presences as well. I’m beginning to think maybe I’ve been missing out on experiences or relationships or both by my habit of holding everyone at a distance.

Michael's body pushes itself to cling to life for six hours more. Anne comes in with one hour left in his life for one last check before going home at the end of her brutal shift. She can barely stay on her feet but her drive to see her colleague is stronger. As she squeezes his hand, I see Michael's eyes flutter. She speaks to him to say she's leaving and then tells him how grateful she is to have worked alongside him. He can hear her. Hearing is the last of the senses lost by a dying body. She tells him he has been courageous and compassionate, two virtues any good doctor strives to possess.

I watch his spirit rise higher as the times between his breaths lengthen. His threads glisten as that of any spirit who has faithfully served in this world. As his body releases his spirit completely, I notice Gelion has come to float beside me with the spirit she has been tending. Her charge left its body fourteen minutes ago but wanted to stay.

Michael's spirit looks at me with sadness and then relief before his gaze moves past me. Gelion's charge looks back with grateful recognition and moves forward to embrace Michael. This spirit had been one of the many cared for by Michael.

"Thank you," Gelion's charge says. "Thank you. As terrified as I was when I first arrived, you calmed me with your confidence and compassion. It softened my fear and brought me comfort."

I've done this work a long time but there are still events that are firsts for me, and this is one. I look at the two embracing spirits and am overwhelmed by seeing the effects of human compassion and love. Gelion reaches out for me and I come beside her, wrapping my arm around her. We watch Michael and his patient move forward together, both aware they are not alone and never will be.

18 Dot and John

I hover next to Dot and hold her hand. Her spirit keeps drifting above her, pulling a little farther away from her body each time. The threads holding her spirit have grown a beautiful, shimmering silver, very fine and airy. She is ready and there is not much to keep her here.

Much like the woman by the shore, Dot has been preparing. She spent the last two years deciding who would inherit what items from her and putting her affairs in order. She doesn't have much. Her life has been simple, some by economical circumstance and some by choice. She never needed much in her life. Everything she owns has more sentimental value than anything material.

Each child and grandchild received a copy of a letter typed on her 1930s Royal typewriter, whose font is tenderly familiar to all of them from the many letters they received from her over the years. This one included a list of items she thought would be important to them with a request for them to return the list with notes about which ones they might want. She then decided how to fairly distribute everything on the list and made arrangements for delivery upon her death.

There was no need for me to manifest and see her over the past few days. When she dies, she will know me. My journey with her has been long and unexpected.

My first encounter with Dot and John was when John died the first time. I hovered near him as he walked around his son's house. He played with his grandkids that morning, teasing them as was his way. They giggled and said, "Granddad!" with a playfully reprimanding tone. The two of them had just run off to play in another part of the house when he collapsed: a massive heart attack.

As soon as his body hit the floor hard, his spirit snapped away and floated beside me. He looked down and could see himself lying there. We both watched as Dot yelled for her son, then knelt beside John, taking his hand after placing a pillow under his head. We could hear his son and daughter-in-law running across the house to find us. John turned and looked at me with wide eyes, shocked and frightened. He can't see Malak and the others who have arrived to be present for his family. He can't feel their presences, calming and comforting. He doesn't see Malak steady his son's hands as he presses hard on John's chest.

We heard the sound of smaller feet and watched as the daughter-in-law held the children back. Dot held John's hand as their son, a surgeon, began chest compressions. John looked down on his own slack body, then with pride at his son who was saving his life. He hovered there for another moment, relaxing into the strange calm of my world, while watching the chaos of his own.

The daughter-in-law took the children with her to use the phone and call 911. We heard her giving them directions to the house as her husband continued working desperately to keep his father's heart beating. The few weak threads that held John's spirit to his body pulled him back inside a little more with each forceful push of his son's hands.

I travelled with John in the ambulance to the hospital, seeing his spirit rise and fall again and again. In the emergency room, he rose again to float beside me and looked at me. I held his gaze to reassure him until we heard the "crack" of the defibrillator and his body yanked his spirit back inside one last time.

John stayed in the critical care unit for several days for the doctors to monitor his new pacemaker. Dot sat beside him, quietly reading the entire time. Mostly she was joined by one of her daughters or her son or daughter-in-law. But in the moments when she was alone, there were times when she would look at me. The first four times I assumed she simply happened to have gazed in my direction. Humans can't see me in my natural form unless I choose for them to. The fifth time, she looked directly at me and nodded. I stared at her for a moment in disbelief. She smiled and nodded again and I understood. I knew John would be okay and that it was time for me to leave.

A few years later I found myself hovering near Dot in a different hospital, one closer to their home. She was battling breast cancer and her body was exhausted. I watched her spirit lift slightly a few times, but her threads were bright and strong still. Her spirit was deceptively fierce for a seemingly quiet woman. I knew I wouldn't be needed, but I felt I should be there.

During one of her liftings, she looked at me and smiled, giving me a little nod. I smiled back. I knew she knew me and she seemed glad I was there.

I hovered only a few days, watching as the staff administered chemo and monitored her vitals. The cancer was strong but the medications were stronger. Strongest still were Dot's spirit and will. My last day with her she lifted one last time and nodded at me, smiled, then shook her head. We both knew this wasn't her time and I drifted away.

Four years ago I requested to return when I learned it was time for John's release. I manifested and made my way to the back of a small church, finding a spot in the rearmost pew, squeezing in between a large family and the aisle. As a rule I hate attending church, any church. I get too frustrated listening to human ways of understanding God, how imperfectly they see her. But it was Mother's Day in America and that meant everyone would be on their best behavior. For many churches in this part of the world, Mother's Day is one of the most highly attended Sundays and Father's Day is one of the worst.

At the end of the service, during what these Christians call, "The altar call," I stood up. The family looked at me encouragingly, assuming I was in the mood to be "saved" that day. I shook my head and turned away from the front of the church, making my way to the rear. I laughed to myself at their disappointment at not seeing me "give my life to Jesus" that day. If only they knew. . .

Once I had shed my manifested form, I hovered in the entryway, waiting. After the last hymn and benediction, the people began pouring out of the building, chatting and smiling with each other. Several mothers held their children's hands a little more tightly that day. A few of the fathers looked nervous that they hadn't planned properly to celebrate the hard work their wives do for the family.

Near the middle of the crowd I found Dot and John. It was the only Sunday of the year John would attend church in person rather than watching a service on TV. He knew it was important to Dot, so this was the day he made an exception. They travelled every year to the same fishing camp several hours from their home for the late spring and summer. This church service served as a time to catch up with friends they had made there over the years.

I followed them to their car. As John opened the door for Dot, he stumbled, his hand hitting her rear. She thought he was being playful and turned to see he was struggling.

She asked, "John, are you ok?"

"I'll be fine," he answered.

John grabbed his chest then his body went limp. His spirit lifted, completely separating from his body this time. He looked at me, and then we both looked at Dot. She looked at us and nodded.

"She'll be fine," he said to me. He was right.

A year later, Griffin and I were making runs in a hospital in France. He was there to comfort the family of a man with pancreatic cancer and I was waiting for a young woman with Hodgkin's lymphoma to die. Griffin remembered that I had been with John when he died. He had been the comforting presence sent to tend Dot and her family as they travelled home again.

"Phe, do you remember Dot?" I nodded. "She said something the night of John's death that I think you would want to know. You grew close to them both over the years."

Griffin gave me a knowing but hesitant smile. I guess I have a bit of a reputation for denying any kind of sentimental attachment to humans. I didn't argue that time. He was right. I was changing.

"That night Dot stayed in a hotel room with her granddaughter before driving home the next day. Dot hadn't cried while her son's family had been with her. The granddaughter asked her, 'Grandma, aren't you sad?.' Dot smiled at her and replied, 'No, honey. We had twelve years together we shouldn't have had. How could I be sad about that?'"

In my centuries and centuries of work, I know how rare a soul this is. But after my experience with Dot, it didn't surprise me. I also knew her granddaughter would carry this moment with her as a lesson for her own life.

When I learned Dot's time was nearing, I knew I had to come for her. My journey with them has been long and beautiful. I think I have grown sentimental because I have lost my fear. I want to know how she is. I want to see how her family is managing her death. I care. As much as it surprises me, I care.

And maybe I am a little envious. Walking this road with them over the years, I've witnessed something I can never have. Or maybe it's something I never allowed myself to have. Their love is so beautiful and has carried them over their life together and even continued as Dot has journeyed alone. I need to see it through to completion. I want to be here. I want to be the one to take Dot home.

She has lived well in the years since John died. She has continued to hold her family together and shown each family member a love unique to them and shared her wisdom. Her life changed with his death but her strength and will did not diminish.

Just as it was John's heart issues that returned to take him, it is her cancer that has come again to kill her. Since these are the days of COVID, she requested to stay home with hospice and that is where I wait with her. One of her daughters has become her primary caregiver and never leaves the house. Kényelem has come to be with the daughter. She and I are new to each other. I've known her for just a few years. She's a new comforting presence but has a very ancient way about her, as though she came into being with the wisdom of elders. She sees things others cannot and intuits deeper meanings and truths than any other novice I've known.

Nurses come and go to make sure she's comfortable and the daughter tends to her. She has held up Dot's tablet several times for children, grandchildren, and great grandchildren to say their, "goodbyes." It's both beautiful and excruciating to watch the faithfulness of this daughter as she understands the weight of the work she has chosen to undertake out of love for her mother and her family. Kényelem floats around the house with the daughter.

Every friend and family member who wanted to call has done so. Dot has held on to her body long enough to give everyone else a sense of closure; at least, in as much as it is possible during these pandemic times. She has been ready to move on for over a week, but she would not leave until the others were more ready to let her go.

Even now, she waits for her daughter to leave the room. I watch her spirit rise higher and higher but not yet break free. Her daughter has been reading to her and Dot can hear her voice. She also hears it when the daughter stands and walks out of the room for a glass of water. Kényelem looks at me, then at Dot. She knows this is the end and the daughter will need her. As they move out of sight, the last silvery thread releases. Dot rises and turns to me. smiling. Then we both look as John arrives with Hái. It is a matter of seconds before their spirits are intertwined and indistinguishable from one another.

19 Last Run

I am called to Florida. The pandemic has spread, as we anticipated. I assume I am here for another COVID patient. I've made so many runs with victims of the disease that I have lost count and almost lost any sense of location. These have been busy days. Dot's death was the last run I have made during which I felt any sort of normality. Things are beginning to blur for me and I'm spending more time reflecting on those I have transitioned than I ever have before.

I can see the large hospital before me. It's the type that has been added onto again and again with wings jutting off the main building at odd angles. I'm lost in thought as I float down so, at first, I don't notice the police cars. It's the big black SUVs that catch my attention. When I see them I know there is deep trouble, especially if they have blue lights running behind the tinted windows.

As I drift past an officer in a thick black vest, I hear the chatter on his radio. It sounds as though there is a hostage situation on the fourth floor. A former employee has the whole floor on lockdown, threatening them with an assault rifle. Confusion surges through me as well as anger. With all of the suffering in the world, especially now, why would any human choose to create more chaos and pain?

I must be here to wait and see what he decides to do. The comforting presences have created a circle around the officers, drifting with them as they dart from car to car, talking on phones and radios to try to come up with a solution. I hope they come up with something, so I won't be needed.

I enter the fourth floor hallway near the nurses' station and spot him, the shooter. He is neatly dressed with a jacket and button-up shirt tucked into his black pants. In his confusion this morning he put on blue socks and one black shoe with one brown shoe. In a different time it would be the only thing about him that seems strange in any way. But now it's strange to see him dressed so normally, without a mask of any kind to cover his face.

Everything that happens next is a blur and only takes thirty seconds.

Griffin and Mariah slide to either side of me and I turn to them in confusion as they place their hands on my shoulders. At the same time Moébé appears at the end of the hallway, a look of apology and sadness on his face as his eyes meet mine before they turn to the door to the stairwell. I look in time to see Anne walk through the door and into the path of the gunman. He doesn't hesitate to pull the trigger, assuming she's a team of officers rushing in to arrest him. Bullets spray towards her and shred her white lab coat before exploding into her chest. A nurse jumps on the gunman from behind and tackles him to the floor as I watch Anne's body crash to her knees. Before her chest and face fall to the ground, her eyes register surprise, and I know she sees me.

That's the moment I realize I'm not here on a run. I'm here for her—to be her companion on her journey. Moébé catches her spirit as it rises and Griffin and Mariah take me to her. She grabs Moébé with one hand then reaches for me. "Phe," she whispers as I take her arm. "Anne, grandmother of Jesus," I say as I turn to her and prepare for a journey I have never taken.

Acknowledgements

This work is the product of several years. I am grateful for my family for supporting and encouraging me in all of my endeavors, especially writing. My parents have read most of everything I have written, starting with the little lines I punched out on my dad's office typewriter to the vignettes I post on my blog, and have been excellent cheerleaders. My husband, Derek, patiently listens and reads my many musings, some of which only ever end up being read by him. My personal editor, Katerina Katsarka Whitley, has been instrumental in refining my writing to the point I feel comfortable offering it for publishing. She has been a dear friend and mentor. Thank you to my many friends who willingly read my first drafts and provided excellent feedback that helped breathe life to Phe. The final push to pursue publishing came from my best friend, Perla, who has said to me again and again, "This MUST be published!"

A final thank you to the countless individuals and families who have and continue to allow me to be a part of the most intimate moments of their lives. It is an immense honor to be with people as they celebrate and as they mourn. My time with the dying has been the most sacred of my life.